Love Lifts the Curse

Jacoba found herself in a room, the walls of which were lined with books.

Sitting in a chair in front of the fireplace reading a newspaper was a man.

It was certainly not the Earl, because he was young with dark hair.

Staring at her he slowly rose to his feet.

"Who are you and what do you want?" he asked harshly.

He spoke so rudely that Jacoba said, feeling frightened:

"I . . . I have a . . . letter for the Earl."

"*I* am the Earl of Kilmurdock!"

"But . . . but that is . . . *impossible*!"

A Camfield Novel of Love By Barbara Cartland

———

"Barbara Cartland's novels are all distinguished by their intelligence, good sense, and good nature. . . ."
—ROMANTIC TIMES

"Who could give better advice on how to keep your romance going strong than the world's most famous romance novelist, Barbara Cartland?"
—THE STAR

Dearest Reader,

Camfield Novels of Love mark a very exciting era of my books with Jove. They have already published nearly two hundred of my titles since they became my first publisher in America, and now all my original paperback romances in the future will be published exclusively by them.

As you already know, Camfield Place in Hertfordshire is my home, which originally existed in 1275, but was rebuilt in 1867 by the grandfather of Beatrix Potter.

It was here in this lovely house, with the best view in the county, that she wrote *The Tale of Peter Rabbit*. Mr. McGregor's garden is exactly as she described it. The door in the wall that the fat little rabbit could not squeeze underneath and the goldfish pool where the white cat sat twitching its tail are still there.

I had Camfield Place blessed when I came here in 1950 and was so happy with my husband until he died, and now with my children and grandchildren, that I know the atmosphere is filled with love and we have all been very lucky.

It is easy here to write of love and I know you will enjoy the Camfield Novels of Love. Their plots are definitely exciting and the covers very romantic. They come to you, like all my books, with love.

Bless you,

Barbara Cartland

CAMFIELD NOVELS OF LOVE

by Barbara Cartland

A NEW CAMFIELD NOVEL OF LOVE BY

BARBARA CARTLAND

Love Lifts the Curse

JOVE BOOKS, NEW YORK

LOVE LIFTS THE CURSE

A Jove Book / published by arrangement with
the author

PRINTING HISTORY
Jove edition / March 1991

ISBN: 0-515-10536-8

Jove Books are published by The Berkley Publishing Group,
200 Madison Avenue, New York, New York 10016.
The name "JOVE" and the "J" logo
are trademarks belonging to Jove Publications, Inc.

10 9 8 7 6 5 4 3 2 1

Author's Note

THE Scots have always been extremely superstitious, and their curses are part of the history of every great Clan.

For instance, Lord and Lady Airlie have a drummer at Cortachy Castle who cursed the family before he died in 1661.

The drum is always heard as a prelude to another death in the family.

In the seventeenth century, a gypsy, whose two dumb sons were hanged for something they had not done, cursed Lord and Lady Crawford of Edzell Castle with the words:

"By all the demons of hell! I curse you! For you, Lady Crawford, you shall not see the sun set; you and the unborn babe you carry will both be buried in the same grave: and for you, Lord Crawford, you shall die a death that would make the boldest man ever born of a woman, even to witness, shriek with fear."

Lady Crawford died that same day, and soon afterwards her husband was devoured by wolves.

The Scots have every reason to dislike the "Sassenachs" as they call the English.

But the merest hint of Scottish blood brings out the friendliness in them, and they believe that person belongs to them.

I know this very well, as my grandmother on my father's side was a Falkner and a descendant of Robert the Bruce.

My great-grandmother on my mother's side was a Hamilton, so my Scottish blood makes me know that I am, indeed, a part of Scotland, and it is something of which I am very proud.

chapter one

1879

JACOBA looked round the room.

It was devoid of furniture with the exception of two pieces so old and broken that they were unsalable.

The diamond-paned windows looked out onto the garden, and the sun was shining.

It seemed to her impossible that after living in the gabled Tudor house for the whole of her life, she now had nowhere to go.

She had never imagined she would have to leave the village where she knew everybody.

She had to say goodbye to the home where she had been so happy with her father and mother.

At the end of the village ran a long brick wall.

It encircled the estate of her uncle, Lord Bresford.

She knew every tree in the Park, every pool in the wood.

She loved the paddocks where the horses were exercised and the stream that ran through the garden.

They had all been the background to her childhood fantasies.

Then had come a bombshell—there was no other word for it. Her whole world had been shattered when her father and her uncle were killed in a train crash returning from London.

While her mother was alive, her father had been content in Worcestershire with his horses, his shooting, and occasionally a day's salmon-fishing on the Avon.

After her death he was alone except for Jacoba, who was only fifteen.

It was then he began to go regularly to London with his brother.

Lord Bresford, a bachelor, who was only eighteen months older than her father, had always been the talk of the village.

They whispered about his raffish behaviour with the beautiful women of the Social World, as well as the Gaiety Girls.

Jacoba had listened and thought the latter had a certain enchantment about them, something, she thought with a sigh, she would never know.

Her father had talked vaguely of taking her to London when she was grown up.

As the years passed, however, they became more and more hard up.

When her father returned from his visits to London, he would invariably search for something of value in the house to sell.

Jacoba learnt to her surprise that her uncle was doing the same thing.

"How can you sell that silver bowl, Papa?" she had protested. "Mama said it was left to you by your Godfather, and originally belonged to George III."

"I will get a good price for it," her father said sharply, "and I need the money."

"But why? What have you bought that is so expensive?"

"It is not what I have bought but what I have spent!" her father answered. "Everything in London is five times the price it is in the country. You will not understand, but there are women who charm like magnets every penny out of one's pocket."

He was right, Jacoba did not understand.

However, she ceased to say anything even when the Queen Anne mirrors were taken down from the walls.

Finally her mother's jewellery was no longer in the safe.

When she was nearly eighteen she felt certain her father would suggest that she go with him to London.

He obviously could not afford to give a Ball for her.

But she thought he would introduce her to the hostesses, who, according to the newspapers, gave such large parties, Receptions, and Balls every night.

Instead, her father went off as usual with his brother.

He told her to "be a good girl," and that he would be away for only a short time.

She was just nineteen when he was returning from

his last visit which ended so disastrously.

Jacoba could not believe it was true.

The Chief Constable came to tell her that there had been a terrible crash on the railway line from Paddington to Worcester.

Among the dead were her father and her uncle.

The joint Funeral of the two brothers was held in the little village Church.

Their coffins were placed in the family vault.

Jacoba noticed at the time, but did not appreciate the seriousness of it, that there were hardly any relatives present.

The death of Lord Bresford and his brother, the Honourable Richard Ford, had been written up in all the newspapers, especially the *Times* and the *Morning Post*.

Yet only three relatives attended their Funeral.

They were all cousins.

One was a very old man of over eighty, who lived in the next County.

The other two were elderly female cousins who lived together in a tiny cottage near Malvern.

Jacoba knew that her family had originally come from Cornwall.

If there were any relatives living there, she had never met them.

After the Funeral she had little time to think about relatives, only of the mountain of bills that poured in from London.

Apparently neither her father nor her uncle had paid what they owed for ages.

Then the creditors arrived to see what there was of value at Wick House, where her uncle had lived.

His Solicitor told Jacoba that everything would have to be sold.

"*Everything?*" she had asked incredulously.

"I am afraid so," the Solicitor replied, "and I doubt if what we get for Wick House and The Gables will be enough to pay off all that is owed."

Jacoba stared at him.

Then she asked:

"Did you say . . . The Gables?"

"That will have to go too," the Solicitor said, "and, of course, its contents, although your father has already sold a lot of the more valuable things."

Jacoba could hardly believe it.

When the day came for the sale, she could only sit thinking she must be in a nightmare.

The family portraits at Wick House were "knocked down" for a few pounds.

The portrait of her mother which she loved was sold for what seemed a mere pittance.

Even her father's clothes were put up for auction.

She begged the Solicitor to let her keep some of the things she had known and loved since she was a child, especially those that had belonged to her mother.

He told her firmly she could keep only those things which actually belonged to her. Everything else had to be sold.

She tried not to cry as her father's and uncle's horses were taken away by local Farmers.

After the sale was over and she went back to The Gables, all that was left in the house were her bed and her trunks.

"How . . . how long can I . . . stay at The Gables?" she asked the Solicitor, thinking frantically that she had nowhere to go.

"Until it is sold," he said, "and it would be wise if you went to live with one of your relatives."

"What relatives?" she asked.

"Surely you have some?" the Solicitor remarked.

She tried to remember those who had come to the Funeral.

The two old ladies who had told her they lived in a tiny cottage were very poor.

"We would love you to come and see us, dear," they had said when the Funeral was over. "We cannot ask you to stay the night, as we have no spare bedroom, but you are very welcome to come to luncheon or tea."

The old cousin who had come from Gloucestershire was, Jacoba had learnt, living with his daughter, who was married and had three children.

"This is a nice house your father had," he said to Jacoba. "I can see it is quiet and peaceful. I have to put up with so much noise, it leaves me dazed at times!"

Before Jacoba could say anything, he had added:

"I must not grumble. I am too old to live by myself, and at least my daughter and her husband give me a roof over my head!"

Jacoba knew she could not turn to any of them

for help. She was also aware that she had no money.

"Your mother left you what little she possessed," the Solicitor told her, "and it is a mercy your father could not get his hands on it, otherwise it might have been spent."

"How much is there?" Jacoba asked.

"She had invested fifty pounds in Government Stock, which with accumulated interest is now nearly seventy pounds," the Solicitor replied. "But you must understand that when that is spent, you will have nothing more."

"Then . . . what shall . . . I do?" Jacoba asked weakly.

"I believe you have been well educated," the Solicitor replied, "and I am sure you can get yourself some sort of employment."

He thought for a moment. Then he said:

"You are still too young to be a Governess in charge of children and—"

He stopped.

He had been about to say "too pretty," but thought it would be a mistake.

As a Solicitor he was well aware how often young Governesses got into trouble, either with the father or an elder brother of the children they looked after.

He had realised since he had talked to Jacoba that she was not only young, but also very innocent.

He wondered what position he could possibly suggest.

It must be someplace where she would be safe and

not at the mercy of some man who would ruin her.

"I have an idea," he said after a moment. "Why not try for a post as a companion to some elderly Lady? There are, I believe, in the Social World, quite a number who employ Readers when their sight is not as good as it was, and who also want somebody to take their pets out for a walk and change their books at the Library."

"It does not sound very arduous," Jacoba said as she smiled.

"I expect it depends on the person you are serving," he replied. "Some old people can be cantankerous and others are exceedingly voluble!"

He was obviously speaking from experience, and Jacoba laughed.

Then she said:

"It would be exciting to go to London. After all, I have lived here all my life and have seen nothing of the world."

The Solicitor thought London could prove dangerous, but aloud he said:

"I tell you what I will do, Miss Ford, I will look at the advertisements in the *Times* and the *Morning Post* to see if there is anybody asking for a companion. If we cannot find one, I will insert an advertisement for you at my own expense."

"That is very, very kind of you," Jacoba said, "and I only hope that if you find me a place, I will not let you down by being a failure."

The Solicitor thought the way she spoke was very touching.

He was an elderly man and had been married for thirty years.

But he thought with her clear skin and large eyes that were grey rather than the traditional blue she was one of the loveliest young women he had ever seen.

Her hair was fair with little touches of red in it.

She looked, in a way he could not describe, different from other girls of her age.

He drove back to Worcester.

As he went, he asked himself how the hell the Honourable Richard Ford could have got himself into such a mess.

He had always known that Lord Bresford was a Rake and a spendthrift.

However, his brother Richard had been sensible and respectable until his wife had died.

'He should have thought of his daughter when he was amusing himself in London with women who want only one thing from a man, and that is his money!' he thought angrily.

He had not told Jacoba that among the bills which had come down from London there had been quite large ones for jewellery, furs, and clothes, expensive gifts from her father to some alluring creature with rich tastes.

*   *   *

At The Gables Jacoba cooked herself two eggs for supper.

She ate in the kitchen at a table, one leg of which was supported on a brick.

The table-top had warped until there was a wide crack down the middle of it.

The chair on which she sat was also unsalable because it had lost its back and was nothing but a stool.

The broken pieces protruded so that she had to be careful how she sat on it.

She was thankful the stove was a fixture.

There was a little coal left, and plenty of wood in the garden.

'Perhaps I can stay here for quite a long time,' she thought as she ate her eggs, 'and I might find something to do in the neighbourhood.'

She could not think of anyone, however, who wanted a paid companion.

She had a feeling that the Farmers would be embarrassed if she suggested working for them.

Three days later, however, there came another blow.

The Solicitor, Mr. Brownlow, called to tell her that there had been an offer for the house and the estate.

"*And* . . . The Gables?" Jacoba asked anxiously.

"I am afraid so," he answered. "You do see, my dear, that The Gables was originally the Dower House, and therefore my partners insisted on including it with the cottages and the land that goes with Wick House."

He saw the expression, which was one of despair, in Jacoba's eyes and added quickly:

"But I also have some good news for you! I saw an advertisement in the *Morning Post* today which I thought was certainly interesting."

"What does it say?" Jacoba asked.

Mr. Brownlow had brought the *Morning Post* amongst his other papers.

He opened it and read:

"Young lady required as Companion for elderly Peer living in Scotland. Must be well-educated and prepared to enjoy the Highlands. Apply: Hamish McMurdock, Esq., Whites Club, St. James's Street, London SW"

As Mr. Brownlow finished reading the advertisement in his rather pompous voice, Jacoba exclaimed:

"That would mean I would have to go to Scotland!"

"Would you mind that?" Mr. Brownlow enquired.

"No . . . of course not . . . I have always wanted to see the Highlands . . . and I am sure it would be very interesting."

Mr. Brownlow thought privately that she would also be out of the way of the raffish young men she might encounter in London or anywhere else, for that matter, who would undoubtedly behave as her father had.

"I certainly think the advertisement is worth answering," he said.

"I will do that at once," Jacoba said. "We fortunately did not sell the ink or the pen, so I will go and fetch them!"

She flashed him a smile as she ran from the kitchen, and he sighed.

'She is far too young to be on her own,' he thought, 'but an elderly Peer should not be particularly dangerous.'

He had always understood that the Scots were a God-fearing people who kept the Sabbath very strictly.

They worshipped in their Kirks, and they drew the blinds in their homes to keep out the sunshine.

"She should be safe there!" he decided. "And perhaps she will find a decent man who will marry her even if she does not have a penny to her name!"

Jacoba came hurrying back with the ink and a quill-pen.

Mr. Brownlow dictated to her what she should say in her letter, emphasising that she had received an excellent education.

He also made her write that she would be delighted to come to London for an interview with Mr. McMurdock.

However, he must understand that as she was not employed at the moment, she had to ask him to provide her with expenses for the journey.

"Do you not . . . think that . . . sounds a little . . . grasping?" Jacoba asked.

"Now, listen to me, my dear," Mr. Brownlow said. "You have only seventy pounds between yourself and starvation. When that is spent, you will either have to beg the streets, or else come back here and hope that one of the villagers will take pity on you."

"How . . . could I . . . do that?" Jacoba asked. "They are all very poor, as you know, and most of them have . . . no room for . . . their own children, let alone . . . a visitor!"

"Then you must not spend a penny of your own money," Mr. Brownlow said. "Just keep it for emergencies, and whatever anyone asks you to do, they must pay for it."

"I expect the journey to Scotland will be very expensive," Jacoba remarked.

"Then unless they pay your fare, you cannot go!" Mr. Brownlow said firmly.

He repeated his warning several times while he was with Jacoba.

When he left, he only hoped if an answer did come from London that she would be sensible enough to obey his instructions.

When he had gone, Jacoba ran down to the village with the letter.

She found herself feeling excited at the prospect of going to Scotland.

It was not only because it was something new and a country she had always wanted to visit.

It was also because she was finding it increasingly depressing to be in the empty house.

There was no furniture except for her bed and the kitchen table.

She kept thinking of how pretty it had looked when her mother had been alive.

To please her father, she had always picked flowers from the garden.

She arranged them in his Study, in the hall, and in the Drawing-Room.

Sometimes he did not seem to notice.

But she knew it was what her mother would have wanted her to do.

She picked and arranged the flowers even when he was away in case he came back unexpectedly.

Now the rooms were empty.

Dust was accumulating everywhere, and there were marks on the walls where the pictures had hung.

Every time she looked at the mantelpiece she remembered with a little pang the Dresden figures that had stood there.

They had been a very special part of her childhood fantasies.

"I shall feel better once I get away," she told herself.

She thought when she read to the elderly Peer he would want her to speak in a soft, clear voice.

So she practised reading aloud.

Because the rooms were empty, her voice sounded eerie and echoed round the bare walls.

Every day she watched anxiously for the postman to bring her a letter.

She had almost given up hope.

In fact, she was thinking she would have to ask Mr. Brownlow to look in the newspapers again, when there was a knock on the door.

She was cooking one egg that she allowed herself for breakfast.

She felt it would be extravagant to buy more.

There was half a loaf of bread and some butter left over from the previous day.

Yet she could not help wishing she had sausages and some home-cured bacon.

She was just taking the egg out of the boiling water when she heard the knock.

Hastily she put it down on the plate and ran from the kitchen and into the hall.

The postman, who had known her for years, opened the door, and as she appeared he said:

"'Marnin', Miss Jacoba! There be the letter 'ere which Oi knows ye've been awaitin' for."

"Is it from London?" Jacoba asked eagerly.

"It be," the postman replied.

He gave her the letter as he spoke. For a moment Jacoba just stared at it, praying it was what she hoped and not another tradesman's bill.

Then she realised it was addressed to "Miss Jacoba Ford" and must be the answer to her letter.

The postman waited.

Like everybody else in the village, he knew that Jacoba had applied for a position as companion to an elderly Peer in Scotland.

Because they had known and loved her since she was a child, the villagers had waited as anxiously as she had for the answer.

Leaning against the door, which sadly needed a coat of paint, the postman's eyes were on Jacoba's face.

She took the letter out of the envelope and read it.

Then she gave a cry of delight.

"I am to go to London at once and—look—here is a railway-ticket for the journey!"

"Well, now!" the postman exclaimed. "That be good news, Miss Jacoba! An' o' course, we'll all be a-hopin' yer gets the position an' travels t'Scotland, 'though it be a long way from 'ome!"

"I am to go to London first thing to-morrow," Jacoba said. "Please will you ask if anyone is going to Worcester and will give me a lift."

She paused and added anxiously:

"There *will* be someone?"

"Now, ye knows termorrer's Wednesday, when Farmer Willy Hockey taks 's chicken an' eggs to Market!"

"Yes, of course!" Jacoba said. "Will you be very kind and ask him if he will take me with him? And I expect Mr. Goodman at the Post Office will know what trains will be going to London in the morning."

"Oi can tell ye that," the postman answered. "Yer can take th' one as leaves at nine o'clock. Yer don't want to get there late!"

"No, of course not," Jacoba agreed.

"Oi'll tell Willy as yer'll be a-goin' wi' 'im," the postman added.

He walked down the steps.

As he set off towards the gate, he turned and waved to Jacoba.

She knew he would carry the news that she had received the letter from London to the village.

Sure enough, later in the day several of the women came up to The Gables to wish her luck.

They wanted to see the letter with their own eyes.

But what touched Jacoba was that each of them brought her some small gift.

From one woman it was a handkerchief that she had been given for Christmas.

She had, however, thought it too small and dainty to be of any use.

From another it was a knitted scarf just in case it was cold in those "wild Scottish parts."

From a third it was a lucky charm that the owner had had herself since she was a child.

She was sure it had brought her a good husband and three healthy children.

They were all so kind that Jacoba felt like crying.

When they left, she had gone upstairs to decide what she should wear to travel in.

She knew her father would have said that first impressions were important.

She hesitated between a gown that had belonged to her mother and was, she thought, slightly out of date, and one of her own.

Her mother's was of a better material.

It had been made by an expensive Dressmaker in Worcester.

It was a deep blue with a short jacket over a pretty blouse.

The skirt which flared out at the bottom was trimmed with a braid.

"I will wear that," Jacoba decided.

She was not aware that the colour made her skin seem translucently clear.

It also accentuated the touches of red in her hair.

There was a neat, sparsely trimmed little hat that she wore on the back of her head.

With difficulty she found herself a respectable pair of gloves.

"If I look too smart, they might think I am too 'flighty,' for the position," she told herself the following morning when she was dressed.

At the same time, it was with difficulty that she did not change her mind at the last moment and put on something else.

The Farmer carried her two trunks downstairs.

Then she realised she was saying goodbye to her home.

She was saying goodbye to everything that had been a familiar part of herself for the past nineteen years.

On an impulse she ran to her mother's bedroom and opened the door.

It had been a very pretty room with a large white double bed.

Chintz curtains were draped over the windows, while white muslin fell behind and on either side of the bed.

Now everything had been sold including the large white dressing-table and the wash-stand with its marble top.

Yet just for a moment, however, Jacoba felt as if her mother were sitting up in bed smiling at her as she came through the door.

"Goodbye, Mama!" she said in a whisper.

Then she knew, just as if somebody had told her, that it was not goodbye.

Her mother was still with her, still near her, still helping her and keeping her safe.

For a long moment she stood in the doorway.

She felt she could smell the scent of violets which her mother had always used, also the fragrance from a bowl of pot-pourri that had always stood on the window-sill.

As tears came into her eyes she turned and ran down the stairs.

Willy Hockey was just lifting her trunks onto the back of his cart.

They only just fitted in amongst the chickens and the eggs.

She climbed up beside him, and he drove his young horse through the open gate and out onto the road.

There were people in the village to wave goodbye as Jacoba passed through it.

"Good luck!" "God to with you!" "Come back soon!" they shouted after her.

By the time they reached the end of the village she had to wipe the tears from her cheeks.

"Now, don't yer be upsettin' yerself, Miss Jacoba," the Farmer said. "If things goes wrong and that there Scotland ain't all ye expects it t'be, yer come 'ome."

"If I did . . . where could I go?" Jacoba asked.

"We'll find summat," the Farmer said. "If it be only a tent in a back-garden it's better t'be wi' people ye wishes."

Because he spoke so kindly, Jacoba found it even harder to control her tears.

By the time they reached Worcester, she was composed, and when he set her down at the station and carried her trunks in, she thanked him profusely.

When the trunks were stacked he said:

"Now yer tak good care o' yerself, an' don't yer be gettin' into any trouble."

"I will certainly try not to do that!" Jacoba replied.

"An' be careful who yer trusts," the Farmer went on. "There be men—and men! Some of 'em ain't no good, whatever they tell ye about themselves!"

"I will be careful," Jacoba promised.

He drove away and as she walked onto the platform she began to feel frightened.

She had never travelled alone, and only two or three times had she been on a train.

Then it was with her father for just a short distance to somewhere else in the County.

Now she could not help being vividly aware that it was a train that had killed him and shattered her own life.

'Perhaps I shall never reach London,' she thought.

Then she told herself she was being very stupid.

The newspaper reports of her uncle's and her father's death had said how very few bad accidents there had been since the railways had been developed.

But when the train came puffing into the station it seemed to Jacoba like a huge animal.

It was with some difficulty that she prevented herself from running away and saying she would find something else to do.

Then as she was looking frightened and lost, a kindly porter asked:

"Yer all on yer own, Miss?"

"Y-yes . . . I am."

"Oi'll find ye a seat," he said, "an' Oi'd best put ye in th' 'Ladies Only' compartment."

"Oh, yes, please," Jacoba answered.

He opened the door of a carriage, and as she climbed in he said:

"Oi'll put yer trunks in th' luggage-van."

She realised she should tip him and, looking into her purse, gave him six pence.

He thanked her so profusely that she wondered if she had been over-generous and given him too much.

"I must be careful with my money, as Mr. Brownlow said," she admonished herself.

She sat down in a corner-seat, aware that there were two other women in the carriage.

One of them had a large basket beside her covered with a checked cloth.

It was then for the first time that Jacoba realised she should have brought her luncheon with her.

It had never entered her head, and because she had left the house early, she had had only a cup of tea.

She knew that before they reached London she would undoubtedly be very hungry.

"I was very stupid not to realise I would need food!" she told herself.

She suspected from what her father had told her that the train would stop at several stations on the way.

She would therefore be able to buy herself something to eat.

Then she told herself severely that this was an extravagance that she could not afford.

As the Guard blew his whistle and the train began to move, she waved to the porter who had looked after her.

Then she tried to enjoy the first long journey she had ever taken on her own.

She was going, she thought, from the world that she knew well and which she had loved for nineteen years into another world.

It was one of which she knew nothing, and which was undoubtedly very frightening.

chapter two

THE door opened and the Butler announced:

"Mr. Hamish McMurdock, M'Lord!"

The Viscount Warren, who was reading the newspaper, put it down and got to his feet.

"Hello, Hamish!" he said. "Is she really coming?"

"I sent her a letter enclosing her railway ticket," Hamish McMurdock replied, "and I had an answer yesterday to say she would be arriving at Paddington at three o'clock."

The Viscount laughed.

He was a good-looking young man who had already stirred a number of hearts in Mayfair.

He and Hamish McMurdock had been at Eton together.

They enjoyed the gaieties and delights of London in a way which made them the envy of many of their friends.

It had been nearly a fortnight previously when

Hamish had gone into Whites to find the Viscount.

He had thrown himself down petulantly in a leather chair beside him.

"I am glad you are back," the Viscount remarked. "Did you enjoy yourself in Scotland?"

"*Enjoy* myself?" Hamish replied. "Of all the idiotic, overbearing, irritating men, my uncle is the worst!"

The Viscount poured him out a glass of champagne and said sympathetically:

"You mean he rejected your idea?"

"Of course he rejected it," Hamish said, "I suppose really I was a fool to waste money by going all that way to suggest such a scheme."

The Viscount, who had been pessimistic from the first, was kind enough not to say "I told you so!"

He had, in fact, thought it a very good idea of Hamish's.

It was that the lobsters and crabs which bred in profusion in the estuary of the Earl of Kilmurdock's river should be brought to London and sold.

There was a great demand for them.

Hamish's idea was that they should form a company and sell what at the moment was enjoyed by no one except his uncle.

"I have never eaten better lobsters or larger crabs!" he told the Viscount. "And, of course, the salmon in the river are abundant. But because my uncle has become almost a recluse, there are few fishermen there except him."

He had been so enthusiastic that the Viscount had begun to think it was a possibility.

They had discussed the matter with one or two of the older members of the Club, who gave it their approval.

Hamish had therefore gone to Scotland full of hope.

The Earl of Kilmurdock was head of the Clan, and the scheme would be to the advantage of everybody in that part of the Highlands.

Hamish drank some champagne before he said:

"You will hardly believe what I am going to tell you on top of that."

"What is it?" the Viscount asked curiously.

"My uncle has become a 'Woman-Hater' and refuses to allow one inside the Castle!"

The Viscount stared at him.

"Is that the truth? It sounds utterly absurd to me!"

"It is true," Hamish said. "He always was a rather strange character, and soon after he left School, my grandfather, who was a real tyrant, insisted on his becoming betrothed to a woman from a neighbouring Clan."

"I suppose in order to stop them stabbing each other with their dirks," the Viscount remarked, "and shooting each other instead of the grouse!"

Hamish did not laugh. Instead, he went on:

"It was something like that. Anyway, because Uncle Tarbot was frightened of his father, he agreed to do as he wished."

"A great mistake!" the Viscount exclaimed. "I would not allow my father to dictate to me whom I should or should not marry!"

Hamish did not bother to answer this.

He knew that the Earl of Warrenton was a rather weak character, and the Viscount, his eldest son, did as he wished.

"Well, go on!" the Viscount said. "What happened?"

"According to what my father told me, the marriage was a catastrophe from the moment the wedding had taken place."

He laughed as he added:

"My Father always said that they fought more ferociously and vindictively than ever their Clans had."

"So what happened?" the Viscount enquired.

"The Bride was providentially drowned in a storm that blew up when she was fishing out to sea."

He made a gesture with his hand as he said:

"Why the devil she should want to catch cod when she could catch salmon Heaven only knows!"

"But she was drowned," the Viscount said.

"She was drowned, and of course people alleged that her husband had drowned her in one of their many quarrels. But he had a fool-proof alibi, although he certainly did not mourn his Bride!"

"I can understand his feelings," the Viscount said, "but what has happened now?"

"Apparently a year ago, although I was not aware of it at the time," Hamish answered, "Uncle Tarbot fell in love!"

"Who was she this time?" the Viscount enquired.

"A Scottish girl whom he met in Edinburgh, and I understand they became secretly engaged."

"Why secretly?"

"Because her father, who is Chieftain of his Clan, had never been on speaking-terms with the Kilmur-docks."

"When I hear what goes on in your native country," the Viscount said, "I thank God I was born in England!"

"I suppose we are a rather fiery race!" Hamish admitted. "Anyway, this woman told Uncle Tarbot that she loved him and was sure her father would relent and give them his blessing."

"But I suppose he did nothing of the sort!" the Viscount remarked.

"On the contrary," Hamish said, "the Chieftain did relent and I understand Uncle Tarbot went to stay with him to discuss the date he should marry his daughter."

The Viscount refilled his friend's glass with champagne.

At the same time, he was listening intently.

"At the last minute," Hamish said dramatically, "when everything was arranged, the Bride ran away with another man!"

"I can hardly believe it!" the Viscount exclaimed.

"Well, she did, and you can imagine what Uncle Tarbot felt after his first marriage had been a failure."

"If you ask me, he was well out of it with a woman who could change her mind in that callous manner!" the Viscount suggested.

"You could hardly expect him to feel like that! As a result, he has now become violently antagonistic to all women and has forbidden them to enter the Castle."

"*All* women?" the Viscount questioned.

"Anything in petticoats is barred," Hamish answered. "There are men to sweep the floors, to cook, and to look after Uncle Tarbot with a great deal of pomp and ceremony. But no woman may put a foot across the threshold."

The Viscount leant back in his chair and laughed.

"I have never heard such a thing! It is like something out of a Play."

"It is serious enough, I can tell you," Hamish said. "He is so bitter about them that when inadvertently I mentioned my sister to him, he nearly bit my head off!"

"It sounds as if he is slightly nutty!" the Viscount remarked. "How old is he, by the way?"

"He is comparatively young," Hamish replied, "which makes it all the worse. My grandfather married for the third time when he was an elderly man because although he had two daughters, there was no heir."

"Such things happen to the best of people," the Viscount remarked.

"Uncle Tarbot was born when he was nearly sixty," Hamish continued as if his friend had not spoken, "and he was, I suppose, spoilt from the moment he was born."

"You have still not told me how old he is," the Viscount said.

"I think he is just thirty-three."

The Viscount stared at his friend.

"Then why was your father not the heir to the Earldom and then you?"

Hamish smiled.

"I thought you were aware, having known me for so long, that my father was only the stepson of the old Earl. He was the son of his second wife by her previous marriage."

The Viscount looked puzzled, but Hamish went on:

"Because my grandmother had been married to his cousin and our surnames were the same, he more or less adopted me. I think actually he pretended to himself that I was his real son."

He took a sip of his champagne before he said:

"I was very fond of the old man, and as my father died when I was only fourteen, I began to think of myself as one day being the Chieftain of the Clan."

"But your grandmother died," the Viscount said in a sympathetic voice.

"She died," Hamish said, "and then my grandfather, as I always called him, married for the third time and produced at what seemed almost his dying gasp the longed-for heir."

"I have never heard of anything so complicated," the Viscount exclaimed. "When you talked about your uncle—really step-uncle, I suppose—I always imagined him as being at least fifty!"

"That is what he seems to me," Hamish answered, "and to tell you the truth, I find him rather frightening!"

He drank a little more champagne. Then he said:

"At the same time, I am furious with him for being so disagreeable about my scheme for the lobsters and

29

crabs. I can tell you one thing: I am not going near that gloomy Castle again!"

He paused before he added:

"Thank God my mother's relatives can provide me with all the fishing and shooting I require, only unfortunately they are not on the sea."

"It is very annoying, I agree," the Viscount said.

"I had really set my heart on making some money for a change," Hamish said, "and it would have been interesting to organise the transport of the lobsters by train to London so that they came while they were still alive. They would certainly be in great demand in Clubs like this."

"That is true enough," the Viscount agreed. "At the same time, there is nothing you can do about it."

"I suppose not," Hamish said sullenly, "but the Earl—I refuse to call him 'uncle' in future—need not have been quite so aggressive about it. Nor need he make what is a very attractive Castle into a tomb of gloom!"

The Viscount laughed.

"Are you thinking of taking your revenge on him in true Scottish fashion?"

"I would if I could!" Hamish replied. "The difficulty is to know what I can do, short of physical violence."

"I should avoid that," the Viscount warned. "You know as well as I do that the Clansmen will follow him into battle, even though you do wear the same tartan!"

"He has a fine estate," Hamish said as if he were

talking to himself, "one of the best salmon rivers in Scotland and, according to what he said to me, all the money he needs."

"That must be because he has no women to help him spend it!" the Viscount said cynically. "And it is doubtful, Hamish, if you will be able to afford that pretty little creature from the Gaiety without the money you expected to make from your lobsters and crabs."

"I have been thinking that all the way down from Scotland," Hamish said. "Damn the Earl—damn him —for refusing to listen to what was a sound idea!"

"Perhaps you will think of another one," the Viscount suggested.

"I doubt it," Hamish replied. "And I am certain if we could have got the thing going, the whole Clan would have benefitted. Their Chieftain may be rich, but many of them find it difficult to make any money, especially when there are not the number of fishermen there should be on the river."

"They are employed as gillies," the Viscount said, "and they get good tips in the shooting season."

"They will not get that if there are no shooting parties," Hamish replied.

"Your uncle is hardly likely to dispense with those," the Viscount remarked.

"I would not be too sure," Hamish said. "I think he has gone a bit off his rocker, and intends to live the life of a monk, or a hermit."

"As he is so young, I do not suppose that will last for ever," the Viscount answered. "Perhaps some woman will drop down on him out of a balloon, or swim in from the sea when he is least expecting it."

There was silence. Then Hamish turned to look at his friend.

"You have just given me an idea!"

"Not another one!" the Viscount groaned.

"It is not an idea for making money, but to have my revenge on the man I used to call my uncle."

The Viscount laughed.

"I thought you would insist on stabbing back sooner or later."

"That is the right word!" Hamish said. "Do you know what I am going to do?"

"I am waiting for you to tell me," the Viscount said.

"I am going to send the mournful Earl a pretty woman with my compliments."

The Viscount stared at him.

"You cannot do that!"

"Why not? If she just arrives, not from a balloon or from the sea, he will have to speak to her and, as there is only one train a day, he will have to put her up for the night."

"You are not serious?" the Viscount asked.

"I certainly am!" Hamish replied. "He was pretty rude to me. He scoffed at my idea and said that as long as he was the Chieftain he was not going into trade, however much I might like to lower myself by doing so!"

"I suppose that is the sort of attitude he can afford to take," the Viscount said.

"He may be able to afford it, but I cannot! I need money, and I would certainly like to hit back at a Scotsman who has hit me."

"And how do you propose to set about it?" the Viscount asked.

There was silence for some minutes until Hamish said:

"I suppose I could go to a Domestic Bureau, although it might be difficult to explain exactly what I wanted."

"I should think it would be easier to advertise," the Viscount suggested.

"That is it!" Hamish exclaimed. "You have 'hit the nail on the head'! I will advertise for a young and pretty woman who is willing to go to Scotland."

"And are you going to tell her what she can expect when she gets there? If so, she will not be such a fool as to accept your suggestion."

Hamish thought again.

"I shall tell her," he said slowly, "that I am asking her to be the companion to a man who is deaf, blind, and growing old before his time!"

The Viscount laughed.

"It will be very hard on her when she finds out the truth."

"That *is* the truth!" Hamish said aggressively. "The Earl is deaf to any sensible ideas, is blind in that he cannot see the advantages my plan would bring to the Clan, and he is certainly behaving like an old and disillusioned man rather than one with many years of life ahead of him!"

The Viscount laughed again.

"All right, old boy, you win!" he said. "And of course I will help you, as I have helped you before with many of your outrageous ideas!"

"It will give me immense satisfaction to get even with him," Hamish said.

"I am quite certain you are starting a feud," the Viscount remarked, "which will continue for generations and become part of the history of Scotland!"

"I hope you are right!" Hamish said. "And if nothing else, he will know I have made a fool of him, and that is a satisfaction in itself."

He beckoned the Steward and told him to bring him writing-paper, pen, and ink.

The two friends composed the advertisement together and addressed the envelope to the *Morning Post*.

Then Hamish said:

"I have told any applicants to reply here, but I can hardly interview them in my lodgings."

"No, of course not," the Viscount agreed. "However, as my father is in the country, Warren House is at your disposal."

Hamish smiled.

"I hoped you would say that, and any woman would be impressed."

"Let us hope you have somebody to impress!" the Viscount said in warning.

After the advertisement appeared in the newspaper, Hamish waited eagerly for letters to arrive.

To his surprise, when he went into Whites Club

rather earlier than usual, there were only three.

The first two he opened were hopeless.

The first was from a woman who said she was not as young as the advertisement requested, but she was exceedingly experienced with older people and was prepared, if she was paid enough, to go to Scotland.

The second letter was from a Scotswoman who was living in London.

She said she could go only if she were allowed to take her two children with her, one of whom was four years of age and the other six.

Hamish was feeling anxious by the time he opened the third letter.

It was from a Jacoba Ford, and he showed it to the Viscount as soon as he joined him.

"It certainly sounds exactly what you want," the Viscount remarked.

"We will know if that is so as soon as we have interviewed her," Hamish said. "I have already written to tell her to come to London on Wednesday, but of course there may be some other applicants in the meantime."

In fact, there were no other letters.

While he was waiting in Warren House for Jacoba's arrival, he was praying that she would be as good as her letter suggested she was.

The Viscount, who had been out to luncheon, helped himself to a brandy from the grog-tray.

"Do you want a drink?" he asked as he picked up his glass.

Hamish shook his head.

"I want to have my wits about me when I explain to this woman exactly what she has to do."

"If you frighten her, she will refuse to go," the Viscount warned him.

"I am aware of that," Hamish said, "which is why I intend to choose my words very carefully. I have thought also of something else I intend to do."

"What is that?" the Viscount asked.

"I shall pay for only a one-way ticket to Scotland!" Hamish remarked.

The Viscount stared at him.

"Surely you are being a bit rough on the woman?"

"The Earl will have to pay to be rid of her!" Hamish explained.

"Suppose he refuses to do so?" the Viscount suggested.

"Oh, give him his due," Hamish protested. "He is a gentleman! He would hardly allow a woman to starve on his doorstep."

"If you ask me," the Viscount said, "both you and your uncle are creatures from an outlandish part of the world which is out of touch with modern modes of behaviour!"

"What you are saying is that we are primitive!" Hamish said. "That is true. The Scots have always had to fight for their existence, there is therefore nothing effete about us. We are positive, forceful, and very revengeful!"

The Viscount raised his glass.

"Here's to your revenge, Hamish, and may it never boomerang on you!"

As he spoke, the door opened and the Butler in a pontifical voice announced:

"Miss Jacoba Ford, M'Lord."

Jacoba came into the room and both men stared at her.

Hamish was not quite certain what he expected, but certainly no one as lovely as the girl standing in the doorway.

Because Jacoba was frightened, her eyes seemed to fill her whole face and she looked very young, nervous, and somehow unsubstantial.

For a moment no one moved.

Then Hamish jumped to his feet and held out his hand.

"I am Hamish McMurdock," he said, "who put in the advertisement which you answered. It was very kind of you to come to London so quickly."

He shook her by the hand, then said:

"May I introduce my friend, the Viscount Warren. His father, the Earl of Warrenton, owns this house."

Because she felt it was correct, Jacoba bobbed him a little curtsy.

The Viscount thought how graceful she was.

"Will you sit down?" Hamish said, indicating the sofa.

"Perhaps you would like some refreshment?" the Viscount suggested. "May I offer you a glass of wine, or perhaps some sherry?"

"I would be very grateful for a glass of water," Jacoba replied.

She was in fact very thirsty and also hungry.

She had watched the lady in the corner of the carriage eat an enormous luncheon of cold chicken, pork-pie, cheese, and fruit.

Although there was food and fruit left in the basket when she had finished, she had not offered Jacoba so much as a plum.

They had been alone for the last two hours before they reached London.

She had turned over and over in her mind whether she should be brave and ask if she could just have one of the biscuits the lady had not eaten with her cheese.

Then she had thought it would be very embarrassing if she said no.

She had instead looked out of the window and tried not to think of food.

The Viscount brought her a glass of water which she drank gratefully.

"Now, what we have to discuss," Hamish said when she put the nearly empty glass down on the small table beside her, "is how soon you can go to Scotland."

"I . . . I am ready to . . . do so . . . at once," Jacoba replied.

She saw that Hamish looked surprised and she explained:

"My parents are dead and my home has been sold, so I have . . . nowhere to go."

"And you have nowhere to stay in London tonight?" Hamish asked.

"I . . . I thought," Jacoba said hesitatingly,

"and . . . perhaps it was . . . foolish of me . . . that I would be able to start the journey to Scotland . . . right away."

Hamish hesitated.

"I was hoping," he said, "that you could go tomorrow. There is a train leaving King's Cross at nine twenty-three in the morning which goes direct to Edinburgh. From there it is a short journey by train to Glasgow, where you will have to change onto the West Highland Railway."

Jacoba drew in her breath.

Both men were aware that she was finding it rather frightening.

"I am sure there will not be any difficulty," Hamish said quickly, "and I will buy you a ticket straight through to Inverglen, which is the nearest station to the Castle, which is where my uncle lives."

"It is your . . . uncle to whom I am to be . . . companion?" Jacoba asked.

"Yes, my uncle!" Hamish said firmly. "He is the Earl of Kilmurdock and is very much in need of a companion, so I am sure you will suit him admirably."

"I . . . I will do my best," Jacoba said, "and I have had some experience in dealing with elderly people."

She was thinking, as she spoke, of the pensioners in the cottages who were really her uncle's responsibility.

But because Lord Bresford spent so much time in London, her mother had looked after them.

When her mother died she had carried on listening to their complaints, giving them herbs for their ailments just as her mother had done.

"That is all I wanted to know," Hamish said, "and I am sure you will find Scotland very interesting, if you have not been there before."

"I have always longed to visit it," Jacoba said.

"Then this is your opportunity," he replied.

There was silence, until the Viscount said unexpectedly:

"I think, Hamish, you should tell Miss Ford what salary she can expect from your uncle."

"Yes, of course," Hamish said quickly, knowing that his friend was teasing him.

Looking directly at Jacoba, he said:

"I am certain you will have no difficulty in arranging a reasonable sum with my uncle, who is a wealthy man, and I will give you a First Class ticket and five pounds for tips and any food you may require on the journey."

"Thank you, thank you very much," Jacoba answered.

She had counted her money before she left home and only hoped it would be enough if she had to stay the night.

Mr. Brownlow had been so insistent she must not touch the money her mother had left her, which was invested.

She had therefore thought she could manage on what was left of the house-keeping money.

Her father had given her a larger sum than usual because he had expected to be away for several weeks.

Actually he had been on his way back sooner than that.

She had, of course, been expected to provide food for the three elderly relatives who had attended his Funeral and also feed herself.

Mr. Brownlow had been kind enough to pay what she owed in the village.

She had finally been left with just over two pounds in cash.

She had, however, been obliged to spend two shillings of it on taking a cab from Paddington to Warren House.

It had seemed extravagant, and she would have preferred to walk.

But she knew that Mr. McMurdock was expecting her at three o'clock and she would have undoubtedly been late arriving.

Besides this, she did not know the way there.

It had also struck her that if she were late, another applicant who was punctual might be accepted. Then she would be sent away as soon as she arrived.

"What we have to decide now," Hamish was saying, "is where you can stay the night. Have you any friends who will be expecting you?"

"I know no one in London," Jacoba replied, "and in fact, I have never been here before."

Hamish looked at the Viscount, who realised he was expected to come to the rescue.

"I am sure my father's Housekeeper can look after you for to-night, Miss Ford," he said, "and I know you will be quite comfortable."

"You mean . . . I can stay . . . here?" Jacoba asked.

There was a little lilt in her voice which told the two friends that she was excited at the prospect.

"I will make arrangements for you to do so," the Viscount said, "and I hope, Miss Ford, that you will dine with Mr. McMurdock and myself."

"Thank you . . . thank you very much!" Jacoba said. "That will be very . . . exciting."

She thought with relief that she would not have to pay for her dinner.

With the five pounds that Mr. McMurdock had promised her, she would have plenty of money left when she reached Scotland.

The Viscount left the room and Hamish said:

"I am very grateful to you, Miss Ford, for accepting this situation."

"You must have had many other people who wished to do so," Jacoba said.

"Not so many," Hamish replied. "I think most young women are not keen to take such a long journey to the North of Scotland. But I have just come back from there myself, and the trains are comfortable, and there is seldom an accident."

Jacoba gave a little shiver.

She knew that whatever this Gentleman might say she was frightened.

It was a train that had killed her father and uncle.

"I have to be brave," she told herself, "because if I do not go to Scotland, it may be difficult to find another position."

She had, although she had not said so, been overcome to see how large London was.

And there were so many people, carriages, and horses in the streets.

She had looked through the window of the cab which had brought her from the station and thought that if Mr. McMurdock did not accept her, she would go back home.

She was afraid of being alone in such an enormous City.

But now she had a position.

If she did everything that her elderly employer wanted, she might not have to worry about herself for a long time, maybe until he died.

"You are looking very serious!" Hamish observed. "You need not be frightened of the journey. I will put you into a carriage for 'Ladies Only.' "

"Thank you, I would much prefer that," Jacoba said.

The Viscount came back into the room.

"Everything is arranged," he said. "I have explained to Mrs. Jennings that Miss Ford has to catch an early train from King's Cross."

"Thank you," Hamish said.

"You will be called in good time," the Viscount went on, "and I expect now you would like to rest before Mr. McMurdock and I meet you for dinner."

Jacoba rose quickly to her feet, feeling that perhaps she should have retired before.

The Viscount opened the door for her.

She passed through and found in the corridor there

was an elderly woman dressed in rustling black.

"Ah, here you are, Mrs. Jennings!" the Viscount said. "Let me introduce you to Miss Ford, who is, as I told you, going to Scotland as a companion to the Earl of Kilmurdock."

"I'll look after Miss Ford, M'Lord, and see she's comfortable!" Mrs. Jennings said in a somewhat repressive tone.

"Thank you," Jacoba said again. "Thank you very much."

She walked away with the Housekeeper, and the Viscount returned to the Sitting-Room.

"Well, you have certainly 'hit the jackpot' this time, old boy!" he said to Hamish. "She is the prettiest thing I have seen for years! I can think of far better things we could do with her than sending her into the Lion's Den!"

"Now, you leave her alone!" Hamish warned. "I found her and Fate has turned up trumps!"

"It certainly has!" the Viscount agreed. "I only wish I could see your uncle's face when she arrives blithely at the Castle to be a comfort to him in his old age!"

"I have written the letter she is to take with her," Hamish said, "and I will give it to her after dinner. If that does not make the Earl squirm, nothing will!"

"Doubtless we shall learn after it has all happened just how much he squirmed!" the Viscount said. "But I am rather more concerned with her than I am with him."

"Now, stop interfering!" Hamish said. "When he

44

sends her back, between us we will find something decent for her to do."

"That should not be difficult!" the Viscount said laconically.

chapter three

JACOBA was impressed by the bedroom to which the Housekeeper took her, also with what she saw of the rest of the house.

Her father had often talked about the grand houses there were in Mayfair.

She knew he had been asked to dinner in some of them and had attended Balls and parties with his brother.

But when they grew so poor, she felt she would never see any of the places he had talked about.

Now she looked around.

She wanted to remember the heavily canopied bed, the pictures on the walls, and the thick carpet under her feet.

The large dressing-table with its three mirrors and a candelabrum of silver cupids on either side of it was beautiful.

Her trunks were brought upstairs, and she told the housemaid which one she wanted unpacked.

Among the gowns in one of them were the few special little pieces of china she owned herself and some presents she had been given for Christmas and birthdays.

'Those, at least,' she thought, 'could not be snatched away to be sold!'

She had brought with her her mother's gowns as well as her own.

When the housemaid drew out the two that were on top, she decided to wear the prettiest of them.

It was really an older woman's gown because it was a pigeon-breast grey with little touches of pink round the bodice and hem.

It became Jacoba very well because the chiffon was the colour of her eyes.

It was also a striking contrast to her delicate skin.

She rested, and later she had a bath in front of a small fire.

When she was dressed the maid said:

"Yer looks lovely, Miss, if Oi might say so! It's a pity yer ain't goin' to a Ball."

"I wish I were," Jacoba said, "but to-morrow morning I have to leave early for Scotland."

"It's ever so far away," the maid said, "an' Oi be glad Oi can stay in London."

Jacoba almost wished she could do the same.

Then she told herself she was being ungrateful.

She was very lucky to have a job which would

take her to Scotland, which she had always wanted to see.

However long the journey, she must not complain.

When she was ready she walked downstairs, feeling rather shy.

She was also wondering if it was incorrect for her to dine alone with the two young men.

She had the uncomfortable feeling that if they treated her as her father and mother would have expected, they would arrange for her to have a chaperone.

'I must remember,' she thought, 'that I am a companion, and that is really only a superior servant.'

The Viscount and Hamish were waiting for her in the Drawing-Room.

It was the most splendid room she had ever seen.

It was lit by huge crystal chandeliers and the furniture was French.

She walked towards the two men who were standing in front of the marble mantelpiece.

The Viscount thought no one could look so lovely and not be one of the Professional Beauties.

They had captured the imagination of the British Public as well as the heart of the Prince of Wales.

Photographs of them could be seen in many of the shop-windows.

It would be easy to believe that Jacoba was one of them.

When she reached the two men, Jacoba said a little shyly:

"I . . . hope I am . . . not late?"

"No, you are very punctual," the Viscount replied, "and I think as a reward you should have a glass of champagne."

He put a glass into her hand.

Jacoba, who had drunk champagne only on a very few occasions, thought she must be careful.

It would be dangerous to drink before she had something to eat.

Although she had been very hungry, she had thought it would be an imposition to ask the House-keeper if she could have some tea.

She felt nervous of ordering the housemaid to fetch her some.

When she was alone, she saw there was an elaborate little box by her bed.

It was covered in satin and decorated with a flower made of silk.

She opened it and found to her joy it contained a few biscuits.

She ate them all and they at least took away some of her hunger.

Now, however, she was very hungry, and was afraid the champagne might go to her head.

She therefore sipped it very cautiously and was glad when dinner was announced.

She put her glass down on a table behind a silver-framed photograph.

She hoped nobody would notice she had drunk so little of it.

"I expect you are hungry after your journey," the

Viscount said as they walked towards the Dining-Room.

It was then that Jacoba thought of to-morrow, and she answered:

"I am very hungry because I was foolish enough not to bring any food with me to eat in the train."

The Viscount stared at her.

"Do you mean you have had nothing to eat since breakfast?"

"Only some delicious biscuits I found upstairs beside my bed."

"You should have told us!" the Viscount exclaimed. "Did you hear that, Hamish? Miss Ford is starving!"

"I admit I never thought of telling her she would want food on the train," Hamish replied, "and of course I will arrange that she takes a hamper with her to-morrow."

"There may be a Restaurant-Car on the train if it is an up-to-date one," the Viscount said, "but one can never be sure, and we must certainly see that Miss Ford does not collapse on the journey."

"Of course she must not do that!" Hamish said sharply.

The Viscount knew he was thinking that if she did not arrive at the Castle as planned, it would spoil his revenge.

At the same time, he thought it important that Jacoba should not suffer unnecessarily.

The dinner was certainly delicious.

There were six courses, and at the end of it Jacoba

felt she could not eat another mouthful.

She had never dined with two young men before, and it was a very exciting experience.

Because they were close friends, the Viscount and Hamish teased each other and made jokes at the other's expense in a way that made Jacoba laugh.

At the same time, because she was intelligent, she could join in the conversation, although occasionally there were innuendos that she did not understand.

When dinner was over, they returned to the Drawing-Room.

After they had talked for about half-an-hour, Jacoba said to the Viscount:

"I think, My Lord, as I have to rise early, I should retire to bed, and perhaps you and Mr. McMurdock are going out to meet your friends."

She knew that this was something her father had often done after dinner.

He had made her laugh when he told her how he used to make excuses to get away when a party was dull.

He used to see the last Act at the Gaiety Theatre.

If the Show was over, he would take one of the actresses out to supper at Romano's.

She had not understood what all these adventures on his part entailed.

But she did think that perhaps they were very expensive.

She thought that must have been why he always had to find something to sell when he returned home.

"As a matter of fact," the Viscount replied to what she had said, "my friend and I have no plans for this evening, but we might call in at our Club."

Jacoba laughed.

"My father used to talk about going to his Club. I sometimes wonder what the women do when they are left at home with nobody to talk to."

The Viscount's eyes twinkled.

"If they are as pretty as you," he said, "I assure you they will find somebody to talk to, and it is not always their husbands!"

He saw by the expression in Jacoba's eyes that she did not understand what he was insinuating.

"Ladies may not go to Clubs," he said quickly, "but they have tea-parties at which they gossip with one another, and it is impossible for any of them to keep a secret."

"What sort of secret?" Jacoba asked curiously.

"Oh, unkind things about each other, and, of course, who is in love with whom."

It all sounded very dashing, but Jacoba was sure her mother would not have approved.

She therefore rose to her feet.

"Thank you very much for asking me to dinner," she said politely. "I have enjoyed the evening more than I can possibly say, and I will always remember how magnificent the food was."

She turned directly to Hamish McMurdock as she went on:

"I only hope, Mr. McMurdock, that I will be able to look after your relative and make him perhaps happier than he is at the moment. I will certainly try to do my very best."

She spoke with such sincerity that for the moment Hamish could not think of an answer.

As Jacoba walked towards the door, the Viscount hurried to open it for her.

He took her to the foot of the staircase.

"Take care of yourself," he said in a low voice, "and if things do not work out, please come back here. I promise you I will find something else for you to do."

"That is very kind of you," Jacoba replied.

She put out her hand, and as he took it in his, to her surprise he raised it to his lips.

He just touched her bare skin.

But she thought it was a strange thing to do.

Her cheeks were crimson as she hurried up the stairs.

The Viscount watched her go, but she did not look back.

When he heard her bedroom door shut behind her, he returned to the Drawing-Room.

Hamish was standing in front of the fireplace.

"If you do not feel somewhat guilty at what we are doing," the Viscount remarked as he walked towards him, "I do!"

"I am not going to change my plans at the last minute!" Hamish said in a hard voice.

The Viscount thought before he replied:

"I intend to make certain that when she returns we will look after her, and, of course, apologise for sending her on a wild-goose chase."

"Oh, for goodness' sake," Hamish exclaimed testily, "you are making a fuss about the girl simply because she is pretty! If she had been plain, you would not have cared a damn what happened to her!"

"She is undoubtedly a Lady," the Viscount replied.

"How can you be sure of that?" Hamish asked aggressively. "After all, she appears to have no relatives, needs a job, comes from some obscure village in Worcestershire, and has to earn her own living!"

The Viscount did not answer.

He only felt that he was helping Hamish to play a cad's trick on a defenceless young woman who knew no more about the world than a chicken coming out of an egg.

"I will look after her when she comes back," he told himself.

But however good his intentions, they did not make him feel any better.

*   *   *

In the morning when she was called, Jacoba was told that she was expected to breakfast downstairs.

The carriage which would take her to the station was ordered for eight-thirty.

It was delightful to have a maid dress her and even pour hot water in the basin.

Only when she was about to go downstairs did she remember she ought to tip the woman.

She took five pence from her purse.

"Thank you very much for looking after me," she

said. "You have been very kind, and I am most grate-ful."

The maid looked at the money, then she shook her head.

"There's no reason for you to give me anythin'," she said. "Oi understands yer're 'avin' to work, same as me. I and yer'll need every penny they gives yer."

Jacoba hesitated, then put the silver coins back in her purse.

"It is very kind of you to think of me," she said, "and to be truthful, now that my father is dead, I have very little money, except, of course, what I will be able to earn."

"Then 'Good Luck' to yer, Miss! I 'opes as yer'll be 'appy where yer're goin'."

They shook hands, and Jacoba went downstairs with a warm feeling in her heart.

When people were kind to her, it always made her feel as if she wanted to cry.

At first she was alone in the Breakfast-Room.

The Butler showed her where she could help her-self from a number of silver dishes on the sideboard.

It seemed like a feast to Jacoba, very different from the one little egg she had cooked for herself at The Gables.

Because she thought it was sensible, she ate a great deal more than she really wanted.

She was just finishing her second cup of coffee when the Viscount came into the room.

"I am late!" he said. "With no excuses except that I slept rather badly last night."

He did not add that it was because he was worrying about her.

He thought, in her travelling-gown and the little hat on the back of her head, she looked even lovelier than she had last night.

He put some food on his plate and sat down at the table.

"I have not had time to ask you about yourself," he said. "I am very curious as to why, looking as you do, you have to earn your own living."

"I never thought it was something I would have to do," Jacoba replied in her soft voice, "but I am afraid Papa became very extravagant after my mother died, and so did his brother. Because of it, the house we lived in and the estate had to be . . . sold."

There was a little break in her voice which the Viscount did not miss.

"Was it a large estate?" he asked.

"Nearly two thousand acres," Jacoba replied.

The Viscount stared at her.

"That is large! And you say it was owned by your father?"

"No, his elder brother. But Papa lived in the Dower House and it has been my home ever since I was born."

"Then what happened . . . ?" the Viscount began.

At that moment the door opened and Hamish came into the room.

"Good-morning!" he said. "The carriage is at the door and I think, Miss Ford, you should now go to the station. I am sure you will want a corner-seat in a comfortable carriage, and it would be a mistake to be late."

"Y-yes . . . of course," Jacoba agreed.

She got up from the table and collected her handbag and her gloves.

She had placed them on a chair just inside the door.

The two men followed her into the hall.

Waiting outside was a very smart carriage with the Earl's crest on the door.

There were two liveried servants on the box.

Jacoba said goodbye first to Mr. McMurdock, then to the Viscount.

She thought the Viscount held her hand for a little longer than was necessary.

"Do not forget that if you do return to London, to come here!" he said.

"I will remember," Jacoba replied, "and thank you again."

She stepped into the carriage.

The footman shut the door, and she bent forward to wave as the horses moved away.

As she had shaken hands with Hamish he had put an envelope into her hand.

When she opened it she found it contained her First-Class ticket to Inverglen and a five-pound note.

She put the money away in her purse and kept the ticket in the envelope so that she would not lose it.

She remembered that when she had been dressing, there had come a knock at the door.

The maid had answered it and brought back a letter.

When Jacoba looked at it, she had seen it was addressed to the Earl of Kilmurdock.

In one corner was written:

"To be handed to His Lordship on arrival."

She placed it in her bag and hoped it said nice things about her.

She would have felt frightened when she reached King's Cross if the footman had not found a Porter for her luggage.

He had also accompanied her to the train.

He looked very impressive in his cockaded top-hat and what she knew was the Warrenton livery.

She felt it was his presence that made the Porter find an empty compartment with "LADIES ONLY" written on the window.

He put the hamper, she had noticed with delight, in the carriage.

Then he hurried to the Guard's Van with her trunks.

"I think perhaps I ought to tip him," Jacoba said to the footman.

"I'll see t'that, Miss," the man replied. "'S Lordship told me t'do so."

Jacoba thanked him and before climbing into the carriage held out her hand.

The footman raised his hat before he took it and said:

"Good luck! And take care o' yerself, Miss! Yer really oughtn't t'be goin' all that way on yer own!"

"I shall be all right," Jacoba replied.

She smiled and when he walked away thought again how kind everybody was to her.

She made herself comfortable in the corner-seat facing the engine and put the hamper on a seat next to her.

She hoped the carriage would not be too full.

Then another lady came in just before the train started.

She was middle-aged, plainly dressed, and had a kind face.

She sat down opposite Jacoba, who hoped there would be nobody else.

It was a corridor train.

She thought it possible that people might come from the crowded carriages into theirs.

However, after a great palaver of whistle-blowing, waving of the red flag, and the slamming of doors, the train began to puff out of the station.

"Where are you going?" the lady asked as the train gathered speed.

"I am going to the North of Scotland," Jacoba replied.

"Goodness gracious! That's a long way, to be sure! And are you travelling all alone?"

"There was no one to go with me," Jacoba replied, "and I have never been so far before."

"I should think not," the lady said, "and unless we have a lot of people joining us, we can at least make ourselves comfortable for the next fourteen hours to Edinburgh."

"Is that how long it takes?" Jacoba asked.

She thought she had been remiss in not finding out the length of the journey before.

"Fourteen hours!" the lady repeated. "Unless, of course, we're delayed on the way, as frequently happens."

"We can only hope that does not happen this time," Jacoba said bravely.

She was thinking that fourteen hours was a very long time.

She only hoped she had enough food to last for the whole journey.

She was thankful she had been brave enough to say she needed it.

She certainly could not have gone hungry again as she did yesterday.

She was sure it would be a mistake to spend any of her precious money if it was not entirely necessary.

When a few hours later she opened the hamper she was grateful to find that it contained a thermos-flask of hot coffee.

There was also food enough for that day and the next unless she was greedy.

The lady opposite her also had a hamper.

But she informed Jacoba that she was on a strict diet because she had not been well.

She could apparently eat only things that did not upset her digestion.

This meant that Jacoba did not have to offer to share anything with her.

Although she thought it would have been selfish to keep the *pâté*, chicken, and sliced tongue all to herself.

A Steward came and told them there was a Restaurant-Car on the train.

But when he saw the two passengers had their hampers with them, he did not press them to leave their carriage.

The lady did not talk much.

Although Jacoba enjoyed looking out of the window at the countryside through which they were passing, she felt the day passed very slowly.

When it was getting towards evening, the lady opposite said:

"I told you if we were lucky, no one would join us, and that means we can make ourselves comfortable for a few hours' sleep before we reach Edinburgh."

"How can we do that?" Jacoba asked.

"You can take off your hat, for one thing, my dear," the lady replied, "and I am going to ask the Steward if he can find something on which we can rest our heads."

She put the question to the Steward when he came to ask them if they wanted dinner.

"Well, I don't know about that, Ma'am," he said, shaking his head. "There's beds on the Sleeper Cars, but I didn't oughta take the pillows."

"I am sure you can find us something," the lady pleaded.

"I'll do me best," he promised.

He came back twenty minutes later with two rather hard leather-covered cushions.

Jacoba guessed at once they came from the seats in the Restaurant-Car.

62

"Best I can do," he said, putting them down on the seat of the carriage.

The lady opened her hand-bag and gave him some money.

When he had gone, Jacoba said:

"You must allow me to pay half of what you gave him."

"Now, do not worry your head about that," the lady replied. "Thanks to my husband, there is plenty more where that came from!"

Jacoba looked at her questioningly, and she explained:

"Mr. Corder is a Ship-Owner, and I am on my way to join him in Glasgow."

She laughed before she continued:

"You may think it strange, but I do not travel by sea. If I tell the truth, even before I set foot on a deck I feel sea-sick!"

"That is very unfortunate for you," Jacoba said.

"I manage," she replied. "I am joining my husband, although I would rather stay in London, because otherwise he would get into trouble of one sort or another!"

Jacoba looked surprised, but she thought it would sound inquisitive to ask what sort of trouble.

The lady, however, was busy showing her how by raising the arms of the seats they could lie down on them.

Their heads lay on the rather hard pillows.

"I never thought I could do that," Jacoba exclaimed.

"You will learn! So take off your shoes and, if you think you will be warm enough, your jacket, so that it will not be creased when you arrive in Edinburgh."

Jacoba did as she was told.

After they had drawn the blinds and lowered the lights, she fell asleep.

*   *   *

Jacoba half woke once or twice, wondering where she was.

The noise of the wheels gave her the answer, and she fell asleep again to the rhythm of them.

Then she woke completely to find it was not long after midnight.

"We will be in in an hour," said Mrs. Corder, "and that will give you time to tidy yourself and have something to eat."

Jacoba did both.

Then, as the train came in to Waverley Station in Edinburgh, she realised that she was in Scotland, and had been for some time.

There was no mistaking the broad accents of the Porters' voices as they came to the carriage-door.

"If you are going on to Glasgow to take the West Highland Railway," the lady said, "you can come along with me."

"Oh, thank you," Jacoba said gratefully. "I was wondering what I should do about finding the train!"

"Fortunately we do not have to change stations," Mrs. Corder said.

Jacoba went with her to the Guard's Van and pointed out her luggage to the Porter.

Mrs. Corder gave instructions to the Porter.

Then they walked for what seemed to Jacoba a long way to another platform.

When they reached it, the Porter made enquiries on Mrs. Corder's instructions.

He came back to say that the train for Glasgow was two hours late.

"Just as I expected!" Mrs. Corder said. "It does not surprise me! I have never known it be on time."

"Perhaps you ladies'd like to go into the Restaurant," the Porter said. "They've opened it, seeing your train from London were two hours late. Oi'll look after your luggage."

"Then mind you do!" Mrs. Corder admonished. "I do not want to lose anything."

"It'll be safe wi' me," the Porter replied.

Mrs. Corder took Jacoba not to the Waiting-Room but to the Restaurant.

"I could do with a drink," she said, "and I expect you would like another cup of coffee?"

Jacoba hesitated.

She still had a little left in her thermos-flask, and she had eaten some of the food which had been left in her picnic-basket.

She thought it would be extravagant to buy anything more.

"You are my guest," Mrs. Corder said. "I will buy you a cup of coffee, or something stronger if you like. Personally, I need a whisky."

Jacoba stared at her in astonishment.

She had never thought that any Lady would drink whisky, although she knew it was a favourite with the Scots.

She was, however, too polite to say anything.

She sat down with Mrs. Corder at a small table in the Restaurant.

The waiter brought Mrs. Corder a whisky and soda and Jacoba had some coffee and a hot scone.

"If you have never been in Scotland before," Mrs. Corder said, "I think you will enjoy the national dishes, although you will be sick to death of them before you are finished! But you will begin by finding them tasteful."

Jacoba spread butter on the scone and thought it was delicious.

She thought as there were so many people there that she would have been too nervous to eat and drink.

She had no idea that many of the men were looking at her admiringly.

'The girl is far too pretty to travel alone,' Mrs. Corder thought, but she did not say so.

When they had finished they sat talking until it was time to go back to where the Porter was guarding their luggage.

"Only about five minutes t'go!" he said.

"Will I have to change trains when I arrive in Glasgow?" Jacoba asked.

"Depends where you're goin'," the Porter replied.

Jacoba showed him her ticket.

"Inverglen!" he said. "That's a long way t'go, an'

ye'll travel on the West Highland Railway. It's no been open for lang."

"And you have to change trains?" Mrs. Corder asked.

"Aye, that's right," the Porter replied.

Jacoba hoped it would not be complicated in any way, and when they got into the train Mrs. Corder asked:

"Will you be staying in the Highlands?"

"I am going there as companion and Reader to an old gentleman who is going blind and deaf," Jacoba explained. "He lives in Murdock Castle."

Mrs. Corder thought for a moment.

"I have never heard of it, but there are many Castles in Scotland. You will find one wherever you look, and many of them are in bad repair."

Jacoba was listening with interest, and Mrs. Corder went on:

"Sometimes the towers are falling down with the Chieftain having no money to pay for any renovations."

It sounded rather depressing.

But Jacoba thought that if the Earl could afford a companion, he could not be poor, as she and her father had been.

As the train moved on, Mrs. Corder talked of her husband's ships and the very comfortable house she had on the outskirts of Glasgow.

"If you had not had an appointment," she said, "I could have asked you to come and stay with me."

"I would have enjoyed that," Jacoba said, "and I

am so lucky to have met you."

Mrs. Corder smiled.

"You are a very pretty girl," she said, "and mind you, take care of yourself! Do not go listening to the first young man who pays you a compliment, or tries to kiss you."

"I am sure no one will do that!" Jacoba said.

Jacoba blushed at the thought, and Mrs. Corder said:

"You are far too young and pretty to be wandering about the world on your own! Have you no parents or relatives to look after you?"

"I . . . I am afraid . . . not," Jacoba answered.

"Very well, you will just have to learn to fight for your rights," Mrs. Corder said, "and make no mistake, it can easily turn into a fight when there is a man about!"

The way she spoke made Jacoba feel uncomfortable.

She told herself she would be quite safe with the Earl, who was old, blind, and deaf.

At the same time, Mrs. Corder repeated her warning several times that she must be careful.

When they reached Glasgow she said:

"I am going to put you in the train and make sure you get a carriage where you will be undisturbed. You have a long way still to go."

"I do not want to be a bother to you," Jacoba said.

"I am worrying about you," Mrs. Corder replied. "As I have already said, you are far too pretty to be going all this way by yourself!"

"I have been lucky so far," Jacoba said as she smiled, "in finding you."

"That may be true," Mrs. Corder agreed, "but another time you might not be so lucky."

When they reached Glasgow she sent a Porter to collect their luggage as she had before.

Then she took Jacoba across the huge station to the platform from where the West Highland trains left.

Because their train had been so late, Jacoba was afraid she might miss the connection.

But fortunately the train to the Highlands was waiting.

There were a large number of passengers in the Third- and Second-Class compartments, but the First-Class were almost empty.

Mrs. Corder chose the one she thought best because it was not over the wheels.

As a Porter put Jacoba's luggage in with her, Mrs. Corder said for the hundredth time:

"Now, you take care of yourself, and do not do anything of which your mother, if she were alive, would disapprove!"

"I will certainly not do that!" Jacoba replied.

As she spoke, she looked so pretty that Mrs. Corder felt it was hopeless to try and protect her from the dangers that might be waiting for her.

How could she make this innocent girl understand that because she was travelling alone, whether he was English or Scots, a man would think her fair game?

Then she had an idea.

She spoke to the Porter, who was waiting at the carriage door.

Jacoba did not hear what she said.

He nodded his head and hurried away.

Mrs. Corder came back to the carriage.

"I have asked the Porter," she said, "to fetch the Guard."

"What for?" Jacoba enquired in surprise.

"I am going to ask him to lock you in," Mrs. Corder said. "This is not a Corridor train, and you will be safe until you reach Inverglen if no one can join you."

Jacoba thought she was fussing quite unnecessarily.

At the same time, it was very kind of her.

The Porter came back with the Guard.

Mrs. Corder told him who she was, and he was obviously impressed.

Then he came to the carriage-door and locked it.

Jacoba thought she saw Mrs. Corder slip something into his hand.

Then, as he walked away, Jacoba let the window down so that she could lean out and kiss Mrs. Corder.

"Thank you . . . thank you so . . . very much!" she said. "I do hope I shall see you . . . again one day."

"So do I," Mrs. Corder said. "I have always wanted a daughter like you."

Because she felt she was going to be sentimental, Mrs. Corder turned to the Porter. She told him sharply to take her luggage to the carriage which would be waiting for her.

She put up her hand once again to Jacoba.

"Goodbye, my dear," she said, "and God bless you!"

She walked away without looking back.

When she was out of sight, Jacoba shut the window and sat down in the empty carriage.

"Because everybody has been so kind," she said to herself, "I no longer feel so afraid."

chapter four

It was six o'clock when the train left Glasgow.

An hour or so later Jacoba thought she would have something to eat.

When she opened her hamper, however, she found to her dismay that there was far less than she had thought in it.

She had very stupidly not thought of stocking it up again when she was in the Restaurant.

She ate the little pieces of *pâté* and ham that remained, but what was left of the chicken had dried up.

There was no coffee in the thermos, and she thought she would certainly be thirsty by the end of the day.

She was fascinated by the beauty that she saw as the train proceeded on its way.

She had her first view of lochs, rivers which she thought must be full of salmon, and moors.

It was just what she expected Scotland to look like, and as the hours passed, she sat at the window enthralled.

When they reached Crianlarich her carriage door was unlocked by the Guard to admit an elderly lady who walked with two sticks.

With her was a woman who Jacoba felt must be her companion.

For the next two hours she watched as the companion fussed over the older lady.

She put a cushion behind her back, fetched her a clean handkerchief out of her bag, and talked to her in a low voice.

'I suppose those are the sort of things I shall have to do,' Jacoba thought.

She wondered if it would be very different looking after a man rather than a woman.

On and on the train went.

Finally the old lady and her companion alighted onto a platform.

Jacoba asked the Guard how much longer it was to Inverglen.

"We're a-runnin' a wee bit late, Miss," the Guard replied. "But A' think t'll be aboot mid-day."

Jacoba's heart sank.

She was about to ask him if there was anywhere she could buy some food, but he hurried away to start the train moving again.

He was out of ear-shot before she could speak, and it was half-an-hour before they reached the next station.

She opened the window and looked out eagerly to see if there was a Restaurant of any sort.

It was, however, a small station.

She was sure there would be no food in the one small building where the passengers bought their tickets.

It was just past mid-day when the train pulled up at Inverglen.

Jacoba got out eagerly.

There was no one on the platform but an old Porter who collected her trunks from the Guard's Van.

The train moved on again, and Jacoba said:

"I am on my way to Murdock Castle. Is there a carriage which can convey me there?"

"Murdock Castle!" the old Porter replied. "Now, tha's a lang way awa!"

"H-how long?" Jacoba asked.

"Two hour or more," the Porter replied.

"Then I certain cannot walk it!" Jacoba remarked, trying to speak lightly.

At the same time, she was wondering desperately what she should do if there was no conveyance.

She thought it had been stupid not to ask Mr. McMurdock if there would be a carriage to meet her at Inverglen.

Because she had travelled so little, she had somehow expected that at every station there would be cabs for hire.

The old Porter put her trunks down on the platform.

"There's a mon in t'village," he said, "has a carriage he hires out for Funerals and suchlike. I'll ask him if he'll tak ye t'the Castle."

"That would be very kind of you," Jacoba replied. "Is there somewhere I can wait?"

"Ye can use ma office," the Porter said. "There's a wee fire burning in the grate that'll keep ye warrm."

"Thank you very much," Jacoba answered.

She realised as she spoke that it was much colder now than it had been in Glasgow.

The old Porter, who she found was also the Station-Master, showed her into his office.

It was very small and stacked with miscellaneous boxes and parcels which were either awaiting collection or ready to put aboard a train.

There was no comfortable chair, so he took the one that was placed near the ticket-window.

He put it in front of the fire on which there were only a few pieces of peat.

"I'll no be lang," he said, "but don't worry yersel'. There'll be no more trains for th' next three hours."

He walked away as he spoke.

Jacoba sat down and held out her hands to the fire.

She felt it was a rather dismal welcome to Scotland.

She wondered why Mr. McMurdock had not asked the Earl to send a carriage to meet her.

She was beginning to feel acutely hungry and thirsty.

On inspection, she found there was a tap outside on the platform.

Hoping the Porter would not come back and discover what she was doing, she borrowed a glass from his office.

She washed it out and filled it with water from the tap, then drank it gratefully.

It was slightly brown which she knew was from the peat.

After her thirst was quenched she went back to sit in front of the fire again.

She thought that by the time she reached the Castle she was going to be very hungry indeed.

It was nearly an hour later that the porter returned.

"I've had a worrd wi' Mr. McDonald," he said, "an' he'll tak ye, though, mind ye, I had a harrd time persuading him that ye couldna sit in may office a' night."

"I am very grateful," Jacoba said. "It is very important that I should get to the Castle."

"The Laird's expectin' ye?" the Porter asked.

It took her a moment to realise that the "Laird" referred to the Earl.

"Yes, he is," she replied.

She thought the porter looked surprised, but he said nothing and merely put a piece of peat onto the fire.

It certainly warmed the room.

Jacoba was, however, wondering whether she had time to unpack one of her trunks and take out her overcoat.

Then at last the Porter, who had been moving some milk churns onto the platform, came in to say:

"There's McDonald th' noo, comin' up th' glen! He's a dour man, but sure enough he'll get ye there."

"Thank you, thank you very much," Jacoba said.

When the carriage came to a standstill she saw that it was very old and the hood was split in several places.

However, the horse pulling it was sturdy.

A middle-aged man got down from the box and he certainly, as the porter had said, looked "dour."

Jacoba thought he glared at her before he said:

"It is a lang way t'go, an' it'll cost ye two poonds there, an' two poonds back."

Jacoba stared at him in consternation.

It seemed an enormous sum to her.

She was about to protest when she remembered that Mr. McMurdock had given her five pounds for the journey.

She had spent none of it.

"I will pay it, Mr. McDonald," she said, "and thank you for taking me."

He did not move but stood with the palm of his hand held out.

She opened her hand-bag, took the sovereigns from her purse, and gave them to him.

He did not thank her, but turned away, picked up her trunks, and put them onto the front of the carriage.

Jacoba thanked the porter again for his kindness.

Then getting into the carriage she sat down on the back-seat.

It was not very comfortable.

As soon as they started off, she realised that the carriage was badly sprung.

The road was certainly rough, but the horse set off at a good pace.

Then, when they had been driving for some time, they began climbing uphill, then down again.

Either way it was impossible to move very quickly.

The carriage bumped over large stones or sank into holes in the roadway.

Jacoba was swung backwards and forwards until she began to feel sick.

It was certainly very exhausting.

Finally she saw, still a long way ahead of them, a large Castle.

It certainly looked magnificent with its towers rising above the trees.

She thought it was beautiful, but she was too exhausted to be enthusiastic.

She was only thankful her journey had nearly come to an end.

She wondered if she would be expected to start her duties as soon as she arrived.

If she were, she hoped she would first be given something to eat.

"I shall feel better when I am no longer so hungry," she told herself optimistically.

At the same time, her head was aching.

She wanted more than anything else to be able to lie down and go to sleep.

'I must not think of myself,' she thought. 'If His Lordship requires my services, then I must be ready to do anything that is asked.'

As they drew nearer to the Castle, she could see that it was a very fine building.

It was far bigger than she had expected.

There was the sea on the far side of it and she thought as they drew nearer still, there was a river flowing not far beneath it.

She knew there would be salmon in it, and the moor-land stretched away into the distance.

"It is very, very beautiful!" she told herself consolingly.

Then she gave a little cry as the carriage lurched again, the wheels bumping over some hard rocks in the road.

At last they were moving up a drive that was smooth.

The horse, who had been moving very slowly, now increased his pace.

Quickly Jacoba tidied her hair and put her hat straight.

She hoped she did not look too battered after such a rough drive.

They drew up outside the front entrance which was very impressive with a high portico.

Mr. McDonald climbed down from the box and started to pull the trunks off the carriage and onto the ground.

He had not bothered to knock on the door.

As Jacoba stepped down from the carriage, she thought that was what she must do.

The silver knocker was large and heavy.

She had to exert all her strength to raise it and knock two or three times.

Mr. McDonald had put her trunks one on top of the other.

He was now, to Jacoba's surprise, climbing back into the driving-seat.

She thought he might at least have waited until she had been received inside.

Before he moved off she called out:

"Thank you for bringing me here!"

"Ah've to be back hame afore it gins dark," he said gruffly, and drove off.

Jacoba turned towards the door.

She was just thinking of knocking again, when to her relief she heard footsteps and a moment later the door was opened.

A young man stood there who she thought must be a footman.

He was wearing a kilt and a jacket cut in the Scottish fashion.

He did not speak but stared at her until Jacoba said:

"I am Miss Ford, and you are expecting me."

The footman still stared at her and said with a broad Scottish accent:

"Ah think ye've come t'the wrong place."

"Surely this is Murdock Castle?" Jacoba said. "And I have an appointment with the Earl of Kilmurdock."

She opened her hand-bag as she spoke and drew out the letter which Hamish McMurdock had given her.

The footman stared at it, but she had the idea he could not read.

"Will you kindly take me to His Lordship," Jacoba said, thinking he was rather stupid, "and my luggage is outside."

The footman turned to look at it, then without closing the door walked ahead of her.

Jacoba thought she was expected to follow him, and she therefore did so without speaking.

They passed through the large hall at the end of which was a wide stone staircase twisting upwards.

The footman still went ahead and Jacoba, somewhat awed by the size and grandeur around her, followed him up the stairs.

She remembered as she did so that somebody had told her that in Scotland the best rooms in great houses were all on the First Floor.

It was certainly a very impressive landing with paintings on the walls and a huge fireplace with a stag's head over it.

The footman did not open the door immediately on their left but went on a little way down a wide corridor.

Ahead were some double doors and Jacoba had the idea that he hesitated before opening one of them.

Then, as he did so, and Jacoba walked past him into the room, he said:

"A lady t' see ye, M'Lorrd."

Jacoba found herself in a room, the walls of which were lined with books.

There were two high windows and a large fireplace at one end.

Sitting in a chair in front of it and reading a newspaper was, she saw, a man.

It was certainly not the Earl, because he was young

with dark hair. He was wearing a kilt of the same tartan as the footman.

His sporran was an impressive-looking one, Jacoba was thinking as she heard the door close behind her.

As the man at the other end of the room just stared at her, she moved forward a few steps to say a little nervously:

"I . . . I have . . . arrived . . . and I am sorry if I am . . . a little late."

Slowly the man in the chair rose to his feet.

Two spaniels who had been lying on the hearth-rug in front of the fire jumped up too.

They stood, Jacoba thought, staring at her in the same extraordinary way as the man was.

"Who are you and what do you want?" he asked harshly.

As he raised his voice it took her by surprise.

He sounded aggressive, and it was a second or two before she answered:

"I . . . I have come to . . . look after the Earl . . . as was arranged."

"What do you mean—arranged?" the man asked. "And what is your business?"

He spoke so rudely that Jacoba said, feeling frightened:

"I . . . I think it would be . . . best for me to . . . see the Earl himself. I have a . . . letter for him."

She held out the envelope that Hamish McMurdock had given her.

They were still standing some distance apart from

each other, and she thought there was an ominous
silence before he said:

"Give it to me!"

"I . . . I was told to give it . . . to the . . . Earl
of Kilmurdock," Jacoba said faintly.

"*I* am the Earl of Kilmurdock!"

"But . . . but that is . . . impossible!" she answered. "I was told that he was . . . old . . . and
needed a companion to . . . look after him."

It flashed through her mind that perhaps the Earl
had died and this unpleasant, rude young man had
taken his place.

He held out his hand.

"Give it to me!" he said harshly.

Because she felt it was impossible to disobey him,
Jacoba moved forward a few steps and held out the
letter at arm's length.

He seemed almost to snatch it from her.

Opening the envelope, he pulled out the letter
inside and read it with a scowl on his face.

As she watched him, Jacoba felt frightened.

At the same time, because she had been so thrown
about in the carriage and was also very hungry, she
felt as if the floor were rocking beneath her feet.

The Earl read the letter which Hamish had sent
him.

Then he tore it into pieces and threw it into the
fire and turned round.

"Get out!" he said. "Get out of my house and do
not let me see you or hear of you again!"

He shouted the words at her, and the tone of his

voice was even more frightening than what he said.

"I . . . I do not . . . understand . . . " she tried to answer.

He put out his hand and pointed his finger at her saying:

"Get out, and if you do not do so, I will have you thrown out!"

He spoke so furiously, and his gesture was so menacing that, as if they had been given an order, the dogs rushed at Jacoba.

One of the spaniels sprang at her, snarling.

She gave a little scream, tried to turn, then she slipped and fell.

As she did so, she felt a violent pain in her ankle as the other dog bit her.

A darkness seemed to come up from the ground, and she knew no more.

* * *

Jacoba came back to consciousness, aware that somebody was feeling her ankle.

Though the touch was gentle, it hurt and she groaned.

"It is all right," a quiet voice said. "It is not a very deep bite."

Jacoba opened her eyes.

She was aware that she was lying on a bed and there was a canopy overhead.

A man was bandaging her ankle and her foot was bare.

Her head seemed as if it were filled with cotton-wool.

It took her a few minutes to realise that she was still dressed in the clothes in which she had arrived.

Somebody must have removed her stocking, for a bandage was being put round her bare ankle.

"The . . . dog . . . bit me," she said slowly.

"He must have thought he had a reason to do so," the man said dryly. "They are very gentle spaniels, as a rule."

He looked at Jacoba's frightened face and said:

"You fainted, partly, I suspect, because you were exhausted after making such a long journey."

"It took a very . . . long time to . . . get here," Jacoba said hesitatingly, "b-but . . . he said I am to . . . go away . . . again at once."

"His Lordship told me that when he sent for me."

"Who . . . who are you?"

"My name is Faulkner and I am a Doctor. I can assure you you have caused a great commotion in the Castle!"

He smiled as he spoke, but Jacoba said:

"I . . . I am sorry . . . but Mr. Hamish McMurdock . . . t-told me to come."

She gave a sudden cry.

"He must . . . have been . . . lying . . . he said the Earl was an . . . old man . . . nearly deaf and blind who . . . needed a . . . companion."

Doctor Faulkner finished bandaging her ankle and set her foot down gently on the bed.

"I am afraid that Hamish, whom I have known for

many years, was playing a trick on his uncle!"

"You mean . . . that man who . . . told me to . . . go away . . . really *is* the Earl?"

The Doctor nodded.

"Then . . . I must . . . go away at once! But I am afraid I . . . have no money."

The Doctor frowned.

"Do you mean young Hamish sent you here without giving you the price of your return ticket?"

"He . . . gave me . . . a ticket from . . . King's Cross to . . . Inverglen . . . and five pounds . . . for . . . expenses on the journey . . . I had to pay . . . four pounds to Mr. McDonald for a . . . carriage from . . . the station."

The Doctor's lips twisted.

"So old McDonald was up to his tricks again!" he remarked.

"What am . . . I to do . . . please . . . what am I to do?" Jacoba pleaded piteously.

"There is nothing you can do for the moment but rest your leg," the Doctor replied. "I will tell His Lordship so, and he will just have to put up with you!"

"He . . . was angry . . . very angry that I have . . . come here!" Jacoba said with an anxious note in her voice.

"I know he is sorry that his dogs have injured you," the Doctor remarked, "and they, as well as Hamish, have ensured that you are his guest, whether he likes it or not!"

"I . . . I would . . . much rather . . . leave!" Jacoba said.

"As your Medical Adviser, that is something I cannot allow!" Doctor Faulkner replied. "There is every likelihood, I am afraid, that this wound will swell and be unpleasantly painful for several days."

"Then . . . what can I . . . do?"

Despite herself, she gave a little sob as she said:

"I . . . I am very hungry . . . but perhaps . . . as he is so angry . . . His Lordship will give me nothing to eat."

"Surely you brought some food with you for the journey?" the Doctor asked.

"I had some for yesterday . . . but it was practically all finished when I left Glasgow at six o'clock this morning."

The Doctor looked at her, Jacoba thought, as if he could hardly credit that she should have been so foolhardy.

"Leave everything to me," he said at last, "and all you must do now is to get into bed. There is no lady's-maid here to help you undress, but as I am a Doctor, you will have to trust me to help you."

As he spoke, he very gently helped her to sit up.

He took off her jacket and undid her blouse at the back.

Then he said:

"I am going to find a nightgown in one of your trunks which I will have brought up here. In the meantime, try to take off everything you can without moving your left leg. Do you understand?"

"I . . . I will try," Jacoba said weakly.

The Doctor went from the room.

Jacoba pulled off her blouse and managed by undoing her skirt at the waist to slip it down nearly to her knees without moving her foot.

It was throbbing with every movement she made.

She realised when she pushed down her skirt that the Doctor had cut her stocking off at the knee.

He had not undone her suspenders.

'He is so kind,' she thought, 'but at the same time I am afraid the Earl will be very, very angry!'

She told herself she must leave as soon as possible.

But by the time she had removed most of her clothing and had covered herself with it her head was reeling.

Her eyes were closed and she was drifting away into unconsciousness when the Doctor returned.

Two footmen came behind him, carrying her trunks.

They put them down where he told them to.

As they left the room he came to the bedside.

"I have ordered you some food," he said, "but first I want to make you comfortable."

"I have . . . taken off . . . all I can . . . without . . . moving my . . . foot," she murmured.

"So I see," he replied, "and you have done it very sensibly. Tell me which of your trunks contains your nightgowns."

"The one that . . . has a strap . . . around it," Jacoba said faintly.

The Doctor opened it, found a nightgown, and came back to the bed.

He put it over Jacoba's head and lifted her arms into it.

Then, as she slipped it down, he very gently removed her other clothes.

He did it so skilfully and modestly that she did not feel embarrassed.

He moved the bed-clothes from under her and packed the pillows up behind her so that she could sit.

"They are going to bring you some food," he said, "and you are to eat everything, then go to sleep."

"S-supposing the Earl says I am . . . not to stay?"

"His Lordship cannot say that to me," the Doctor said firmly, "and you have promised to obey me."

"I . . . I am sorry . . . to have . . . caused so much trouble . . . but I cannot . . . understand why he is . . . so angry."

Before the Doctor could reply, there was a knock at the door.

The Doctor opened it and a footman came in, carrying a tray.

The Doctor arranged a table beside the bed and placed the tray on it.

"Cook says he's sorry there's nay more," the footman said, "but he did as ye said an' cooked everything that could be done quickly."

"Thank Cook and say I will see him later to-night regarding any other meals," the Doctor replied.

The footman left the room.

The Doctor realised that Jacoba was lying back against the pillows, looking very pale and as if she might faint again.

He sat down on the bed.

"I am going to feed you," he said, "and I expect you to gobble down everything I put into your mouth!"

Jacoba tried to smile, but it was too much effort.

The Doctor gave her spoonful after spoonful of the soup and she could feel the warmth of it seeping down into her body.

The soup was followed by a large mushroom omelette, but when she had eaten about half of it, she said:

"I . . . I cannot eat . . . any more!"

"That is because you have gone hungry for too long," the Doctor said. "But I want you to drink the herb tea I have ordered for you. It will send you to sleep and stop you from feeling any pain in your leg."

Because it was easier to do what he wanted without objecting, Jacoba drank the tea.

She realised it had been sweetened with honey.

It was delicious, and when the cup was empty the Doctor said:

"Now you will sleep well, and I shall come and see you in the morning. But remember to put your foot to the floor as little as possible, and you are not to think of leaving until I tell you you may!"

"I will do as you say, and I do feel better . . . very much better. Thank you . . . thank you! Everybody has been so kind to me to-day . . . except . . . His L-Lordship!"

She hesitated over the last words, and the Doctor said:

"You are punishing him by staying in the Castle when he had sworn that never again would any woman cross his threshold!"

Jacoba's eyes opened wide in astonishment before she asked:

"Why did he say . . . that?"

"It is a long story in which, of course, a woman is involved," the Doctor replied. "As you must be aware, they are at the bottom of all the troubles that occur to man!"

Jacoba gave a little laugh.

"That is not true! Mama always said that women are the flowers in a man's life . . . or they should be!"

"Your mother was quite right," the Doctor agreed, "but some women are very unkind, and unfortunately His Lordship has suffered from two very unpleasant specimens."

"So that is . . . why he was . . . angry with . . . me!"

"He was angry not only because you are a woman," the Doctor said, "but also because his nephew Hamish has behaved extremely badly, and you are the one who is suffering for it."

"I must go away . . . as quickly as I can!" Jacoba said in a serious voice.

"Not until your leg has healed," the Doctor said.

He got to his feet as he went on:

"After all, you are quite comfortable here. Try to enjoy yourself in one of the most beautiful Castles I have ever seen with certainly the finest views!"

"It is just what I thought a Scottish Castle would look like!" Jacoba said as if she were speaking to herself.

"That is what I have always thought," the Doctor agreed.

He picked up the tray as he added:

"May I tell you that I am delighted to have for a change a really beautiful patient who looks like a flower!"

Jacoba blushed at the compliment.

Then as she smiled at him he walked towards the door.

"Good-night, Jacoba," he said, "and be a good girl until I call on you to-morrow."

He left the room and Jacoba wondered in surprise how he knew her name.

Then she realised he must have seen it on the labels stuck to her trunk when he unpacked it.

"He is a very nice man!" she said to herself. "But I hope I can go away without seeing the Earl again!"

She shivered as she thought of how angry he had been.

She could still hear him shouting at her, and she thought now he was hating her because she was in his Castle.

"Please . . . God . . . let me get . . . away . . . safely!" she prayed.

chapter five

"SURELY that woman can leave now?" the Earl asked as Doctor Faulkner came into his Study.

"I was going to speak to you about that," the Doctor said quietly.

"She has been here for three days," the Earl said accusingly, "and the sooner she goes the better I will be pleased!"

"I am well aware of that," the Doctor said, seating himself down in front of the fire, "but she has no money and nowhere to go."

"That does not concern me!" the Earl said sharply. "Hamish sent her here and Hamish can take her away."

"It will take some time to write to Hamish and tell him to do so," the Doctor said.

The Earl was frowning and there was a pause before he said:

"I want her out of the Castle, you are well aware of that! If she was such a fool as to come here without being authorised to do so, then she must take the consequences!"

The Doctor settled himself a little more comfortably in the armchair.

Then he said:

"I have known you, My Lord, since you were a bairn. I have seen you change from a charming, pleasant young man into a hard and sometimes very disagreeable one, but I have never known you cruel either to a human being or to an animal."

The Earl stared at him as if he were startled.

Then he said:

"Are you really saying that to me?"

"I am saying it because there is nobody else, as you well know, who dares to do so," the Doctor said. "I was very fond of your mother, and I think it would make her extremely unhappy to see the way you are behaving."

The Earl moved a little uncomfortably in his chair.

He did not reply although Doctor Faulkner was well aware that he was longing to tell him to mind his own business.

The Doctor had, however, a very special place not only in the life of the Castle and those who lived in it.

He was also loved by everybody in the Clan, and they would walk miles to consult him.

There was not a woman on the whole estate who

did not want him to deliver her children when they were born.

He knew that was what the Earl was thinking, and his eyes were twinkling as he said:

"Now, come along! You know as well as I do that you will have to pay this child's fare back to London, or rather to the village where she lived with her father and mother before they died and her home had to be sold to pay her father's debts."

"This has nothing to do with me!" the Earl said angrily. "You are trying to make me feel sorry for the girl."

"It was, after all, your dog that bit her," the Doctor reminded him, "and I dare say in a Court of Law she would be awarded damages for what she has suffered."

The Earl looked at the Doctor in astonishment.

"You are not suggesting she would go to Law?"

"She is too young even to think of such a thing, and she is not only innocent but also entirely ignorant of a world which contains terrifying people like yourself!"

The Earl laughed as if he could not help it.

"Damn you, Faulkner!" he said. "You are trying to get round me and make me sorry for the tiresome woman."

"Well, I am very sorry for her," the Doctor said, "and if I could find her a position where she would be unmolested by men and be with somebody who would be kind to her, I would do so."

"If you feel like that, it should not be difficult," the Earl said sharply. "But there is no position here for a woman and, as far as I am concerned, there never will be!"

The Doctor rose to his feet.

"That is what I expected you to say, and in two or three days' time I want you to pay Jacoba's fare back to London, although, seeing how lovely she is, it is wrong for her to travel alone."

The Earl did not reply but rose and stood looking down into the fire.

The Doctor walked towards the door, and just as he reached it the Earl asked:

"Why is the woman called Jacoba? That is a Scottish name!"

"Of course it is," Doctor Faulkner replied. "I have never questioned it, but it is something you might do yourself."

He felt sure the Earl would make an angry retort.

He went through the door quickly.

As he walked down the stairs he was smiling.

He was thinking it was amusing that the Earl, who had sworn never to have a woman inside the Castle again, had been forced by Fate to accept one.

But Doctor Faulkner had no intention of hurrying Jacoba away until he was sure she was really well.

It was not only that her ankle was still slightly swollen, he knew that the shock of what had happened had taken its toll.

She was still rather limp and lifeless.

"The rest will do her good!" he said to himself as he reached the front-door.

*   *   *

Jacoba was in fact glad to be able to get back into bed after she had washed and moved about the room.

What she really enjoyed was being able to look out the window at the glorious view she had of the sea.

As the Castle stood in a valley the land projected on either side of it.

She could see for herself the Northern Lights about which she had read and which her mother had told her were more beautiful in Scotland than anywhere else in the world.

"It would be impossible for anything to be more beautiful!" Jacoba told herself.

She could not help being vividly conscious that the Earl was under the same roof, extensive though it was, and hating her because she was a woman.

Nor could she understand how furious he had been at the trick his nephew had played on him.

She still shivered when she remembered the anger in his voice and the fury with which he had pointed at her and which had made his dogs attack her.

At the same time, however terrifying it had been, she was in Scotland.

'When I go South, perhaps I shall never come back again!' she thought. 'I must remember how beautiful it is and how this Castle could not be more impressive.'

The first morning after her injury she had been woken by a strange sound which at first she could not identify.

Then she realised it was the pipes.

She remembered reading somewhere that the Chieftains in Scotland were always woken by their Pipers.

They marched round the outside of the house, playing the tunes to which the Clan went to war.

Each morning after the first she awoke at the sound.

She thought it was a delightful way to start a new day.

As soon as she could manage it, she had got out of bed to look out the window.

She could see the Piper in his kilt and plaid and bonnet marching below her as he blew on his pipes.

She knew it would be something to remember when she left Scotland.

Although he frightened her, she thought that it would be exciting to see the Earl in the full regalia of a Clan Chieftain.

The days would have passed slowly were it not for the fact that Doctor Faulkner arranged for her to have books to read.

He had sent a footman up with a dozen, with a message there were plenty more in the Library when she wished to change them.

The Doctor had chosen, deliberately she thought, books that were all about Scotland.

She had lain in bed and read of the legends which went back hundreds of years—the ghosts, the curses, and the battles between the Clans.

It was all fascinating.

Whenever the footmen carried up her meals she

would ask them to change the books she had already read for others.

They were too frightened to ask the Earl what they should bring her.

She therefore received a miscellaneous collection, most of which, nevertheless, she found enthralling.

Doctor Faulkner called on her twice a day.

An elderly Scotsman, who she learned had been at the Castle for years and was the Butler, came regularly to ask her if there was anything she wanted.

He was a kindly man and she learnt he had a family of his own.

But because of the new rule of no women in the Castle, they lived in a cottage.

It was a little way from the Castle.

"It must be a nuisance for you having to go backwards and forwards whether it is raining or snowing!" Jacoba said sympathetically.

"Aye, it is, an' I must be able t'walk aboot the Castle at night," the Butler said, "t'mak' sure a's in orrder fray His Lordship. But ma wife is comfortable and the bairns like havin' a garrden o' their ain te play in."

The Butler, whose name was Ross, told Jacoba a great deal about the Castle.

He detailed how beautiful many of the rooms were.

"I wish I could see them!" she said wistfully.

When he did not reply, she knew that was impossible because the Earl would forbid it.

She changed the subject because she did not wish to embarrass the man.

"I must get well," she told herself after the Doctor's visit on the third day. "I cannot stay in this room being a nuisance to the Earl, and I must start thinking what I must do when I go South."

She thought the only thing she could do was to go back to the village.

She would ask Mr. Brownlow, the Solicitor, if he would help her find some other kind of employment.

She felt she could never aspire to being a companion again after this engagement had been such a failure.

'I must think of something!' she thought desperately. 'Otherwise I shall have to sell my investments in order to live.'

She knew that Mr. Brownlow would disapprove of that idea.

But she could hardly impose upon the villagers.

When she thought it over, she could not think of one cottage which was large enough to give her a room in which to sleep.

"What shall I do?" she asked desperately.

It was a cry for help, and her mother and father, wherever they were, must hear her.

*   *   *

If Jacoba was aware of the Earl, he was no less aware of her.

He felt as if the idea of her haunted him.

It annoyed him to find himself thinking about her, not only during the day when the Doctor came, but also at night when he found it difficult to sleep.

He kept hearing again her cry as she slipped and fell down and the spaniel bit her ankle.

He knew it was his own fault that the dogs had attacked her.

The two dogs went everywhere with him.

As he knew, they responded to every tone in his voice.

They knew whom he liked personally and greeted them with pleasure.

They knew too when he was rebuking a servant or one of the Clan for some misdemeanour.

He could quite understand that the fury of his voice and the way he had pointed to Jacoba had aroused them.

They had thought they were defending him from her.

"She must have known what she was doing when she came here!" he tried to excuse himself.

Doctor Faulkner, however, had made it very clear that Jacoba had answered Hamish's advertisement in the *Morning Post*.

Hamish had deceived her into believing she was to be companion to an old man who was both deaf and blind.

Hamish had made this clear in his letter.

The Earl thought furiously that his nephew had certainly taken his revenge.

He knew he had been abrupt and disagreeable about the young man's scheme for selling crabs and lobsters from the river.

He had resented Hamish's impertinence in suggesting it.

Yet he could have been more pleasant about it than he had been.

But, he told himself, there was no excuse for his nephew's response.

He hoped never to see him again.

When the Doctor returned that evening to see Jacoba, he was late; in fact, it was after dinner.

The Earl was coming from the Dining-Room as he was leaving.

"Hello, Doctor!" he exclaimed. "I did not expect to see you here at this hour!"

"I had an urgent call which I want to tell you about," Doctor Faulkner replied.

"Come into the Study," the Earl said.

A footman opened the door.

The two men went into the large room which held an enormous collection of books.

There was a very fine picture of the Earl's father in Chieftain dress over the mantelpiece.

As the Earl poured out a glass of whisky and soda for the Doctor, he looked up at the picture.

"Your father was a fine man," the Doctor said as if he were speaking to himself, "and deeply respected by every member of the Clan."

As the Earl handed him his whisky he asked:

"Are you suggesting that I am not?"

"I am suggesting nothing except that your Clansmen do not see enough of you," the Doctor replied, "and they feel somewhat bereft."

"What you are saying," the Earl said harshly, "is that they would like me to be giving fishing and shooting parties and arranging games in which they can all take part."

"Of course they would like that," the Doctor agreed, "and they do not understand why you are shutting yourself away in this dismal fashion."

He drank a little whisky before he said:

"What is more, the women are perturbed because they think you are putting a curse on them because of their sex."

The Earl stiffened as he said:

"I have never heard such nonsense!"

"You know how superstitious our people are," the Doctor went on. "When one of the women had a miscarriage and one of your Farmers lost a valuable cow, they were certain the origin of their misfortune came from within the Castle."

"Oh, for God's sake!" the Earl said testily. "I cannot listen to such rubbish! If I wish to lead my own life in my own way, that is my decision, and it has nothing to do with the Clansmen or anybody I employ!"

The Doctor finished his whisky and rose to his feet.

"Well, think over what I have said," he added quietly. "By the way, the reason I was so late is that old Andrew, who had been keeping watch on the river, is showing his age. He is stricken with rheumatism and it is really impossible for him to carry on. But he asked me to tell you that he thinks there are poachers in the vicinity, and that somebody should be on the look-out for them."

"What sort of poachers?" the Earl asked.

"Apparently there is a gang of them working their way up the coast," the Doctor said, "and fresh salmon commands a high price in Glasgow and Edinburgh."

There was a frown between the Earl's eyes, and his mouth was set in a hard line.

"If Andrew is unable to keep watch on the river," he said, "I shall have to find somebody else."

"His rheumatism is very bad," the Doctor said, "and I think you would be wise to give him an assistant, perhaps two. He does his best, but I have told him he is not to go out at night until I have seen him again in a day or two."

"I will certainly bear in mind what you have told me," the Earl said.

"I shall be coming again to-morrow morning," the Doctor said, "and thank you for the whisky. I needed it!"

He left the room before the Earl could say anything.

After the Doctor had gone, the Earl stood looking into the fire.

He was wondering whom he could appoint in place of Andrew.

The man had looked after the river ever since the Earl could remember and had made an excellent job of it.

There had never been any serious poaching as far as he knew.

The salmon were plentiful this year.

There was enough water for them to come up easily from the sea.

He knew that farther down the coast the rivers were low.

This meant that a gang of poachers might choose to visit the Tavor, as his river was called.

He glanced at the clock and saw that it was growing late.

He thought it would be a good idea if he went and made an inspection of the river himself.

He went down the stairs, followed by his spaniels, and found a footman on duty.

"I am going for a walk, Alistair," he said, "to look at the river. I shall not be long, so do not lock the door on me!"

"A'll no do that, M'Lord," the footman answered.

The Earl walked out onto the drive.

Turning to his left, he moved through a clump of trees which led to some rough ground and then down to the mouth of the Tavor.

It was a mild night with no wind, and the sky overhead was clear.

A half-moon was creeping slowly up the sky.

It was easy for the Earl to find his way.

He had known every inch of it since he was a boy.

He thought as he walked towards the river how much he loved it and how many happy hours he had spent fishing.

He was nine when his father had given him a trout-rod as a present.

He had caught both big and small fish.

The sport had never failed to thrill him.

The idea of anyone poaching his salmon made him angry.

He knew if Andrew was not well enough to carry on as river-watcher, he would certainly have to appoint somebody trustworthy in his place.

He reached the mouth of the river and started to walk along the bank.

The stars were reflected in the water and it was very beautiful.

He felt himself responding, as he always did, to the enchantment of his own land.

He walked on, feeling, as many Scotsmen have before him, that he would die to preserve Scotland and prevent it from being overrun by the English.

He walked upstream for quite a long way before he was suddenly aware of a sound ahead.

He stopped and listened; the dogs growled.

Then he was aware that something was going on.

He moved forward again and saw the outline of a boat and a man standing up in it.

A moment later he heard another man farther up the river thrashing about in the water.

He knew exactly what was happening.

The man in the boat had a net stretched across the river.

It was attached to a post he had driven into the bank on the opposite side.

The man upstream was disturbing the water, driving the salmon down river.

They swam into the net in which they would be caught.

These were the poachers about whom Andrew had warned him, and the Earl walked forward angrily.

The man in the boat was intent on pulling the salmon caught in the net out of the water.

He threw them into the boat.

In a voice of thunder the Earl demanded:

"What the devil do you think you are doing? Stop that immediately!"

His voice rang out and the man in the boat turned round.

He had a sharpened boat-hook in his hand and he stared at the Earl.

"Stop that at once!" the Earl commanded. "You are poaching and I will have you taken before the Magistrates for stealing my salmon!"

As he spoke, a man lurking in the shadows of the high bank behind him hit him violently on the head with an oar.

The man with the boat-hook rammed it into his shoulder.

The last thing the Earl remembered was hearing his dogs barking.

*　　*　　*

Jacoba awoke to the sound of the pipes.

She recognised the tune that was being played as *The Skye Boat Song*.

'That is somewhere I would like to go,' she thought.

Because her ankle was hurting her a little, she did not get up and go to the window.

Instead, she lay in bed, listening.

The tune gradually died away in the distance as the Piper rounded the corner of the Castle.

The next moment there was a knock on the door.

Before she could answer, it was opened and to her surprise it was the Doctor.

"You are very early!" she exclaimed.

He walked across to the bed and, looking down at her, said:

"I want your help."

"My . . . help?" Jacoba asked.

She had moved as she spoke so that she was sitting up.

"Last night," the Doctor began, "after I had seen the Earl and warned him there might be salmon-poachers in the vicinity, he went out alone except for his two dogs to inspect the river."

"What happened?" Jacoba asked.

"Apparently he must have encountered the poachers and, I imagine, accused them of stealing."

"Did he catch them?" Jacoba enquired.

"We do not know exactly what happened," the Doctor replied, "but the dogs saved his life."

"Saved his . . . life?" Jacoba repeated. "What . . . happened?"

The Doctor's voice was grim as he said:

"The poachers bashed him on the head with something heavy, and he was also stabbed in the shoulder with a sharp boat-hook."

Jacoba gave a cry.

"How . . . terrible!"

"Then before they left they threw him into the river!"

It seemed so frightening that Jacoba could say nothing.

The Doctor continued:

"Fortunately his spaniels had the sense to bark and bark. They were heard by one of the shepherds who came to investigate and found the Earl. He was able to pull him out of the water before he was drowned."

"How could . . . people do anything so . . . horrible?" Jacoba asked.

"The poachers have a bad name," the Doctor said, "and they have certainly left His Lordship in a bad shape."

"I am sorry . . . I am really . . . sorry for . . . him," Jacoba said.

It flashed through her mind that what the Doctor was going to tell her was that she would have to go away at once.

However, what he said was:

"I need somebody to nurse His Lordship, and there is no need for me to tell you that there is nobody suitable nearer than Glasgow or Edinburgh."

Jacoba's eyes opened wide.

"Are you asking . . . me to do . . . it?" she asked hesitatingly.

"I am begging you to do so," the Doctor said. "The servants will, of course, do everything they can for him, but it is not the same as having a woman. I am

111

therefore suggesting that you do what you came here to do: look after a man who has been stricken down and is unconscious."

"Of course I will," Jacoba said, "if you are . . . certain that His Lordship will not be so angry when he . . . realises what I am . . . doing that it . . . makes him . . . worse than he is . . . already."

"We will 'cross that bridge when we come to it,' " the Doctor answered. "In the meantime, can you manage to get dressed and come to His Lordship's room, where you will find me?"

"Yes . . . of course."

Jacoba got out of bed, thinking it was an extraordinary thing to have happened.

But, of course, if the Doctor wanted her, she must try to help him in every way she could.

As it happened, because she had looked after so many old people in the village, she was quite proficient at nursing.

Her father on one occasion had broken his collarbone out riding, and she had looked after him.

It was impossible to get a trained nurse.

In their isolated village in Worcestershire, she had therefore nursed her mother before she died.

Since in the Crimean War Florence Nightingale had made Nursing a respectable career for women, it was possible in big towns to obtain the services of a Nurse who had been trained.

But in the country the only woman who had any medical knowledge was the Midwife.

This was usually an elderly woman who kept herself awake with sips of hard liquor.

She was generally quite useless at anything which did not concern a baby.

Jacoba dressed herself as quickly as she could.

Limping a little, she walked along the passage from her bedroom.

It was the first time she had been out of the bedroom.

She was impressed, as she had been when she arrived, at the height of the ceilings and the pictures on the walls.

She had not gone far before she encountered a footman.

"Will you show me the way to His Lordship's bedroom?" she asked.

She thought he looked astonished, and added quickly:

"Doctor Faulkner asked me to join him there."

"A'll show ye," the footman said.

He took her back the way she had côme.

Passing her own bedroom, they walked a long way farther down the corridor.

He knocked on a door and Jacoba heard Doctor Faulkner's voice say:

"Come in!"

She walked into one of the most impressive bedrooms she had ever seen.

She realised it was in one of the towers, the outside wall being curved and containing six windows.

There was a huge stone mantelpiece beneath which a fire was burning in the grate.

The bed which faced it was exactly, Jacoba thought, the sort of bed a Chieftain should have.

The posts which were of oak were heavily carved.

The canopy was of the same wood and surmounted by the Earl's crest.

Red velvet curtains fell on either side of the headboard on which was embroidered the Earl's coat-of-arms.

Jacoba had only a quick impression of everything before the Doctor came to her side and took her towards the bed.

The Earl's head was resting on a pillow and his eyes were closed.

To her surprise, instead of looking fierce and terrifying, he was young and very handsome.

His face was very pale beneath a slight sunburn.

She thought there was an expression of pain in the droop of his mouth.

Very gently the Doctor moved back the sheets which covered him.

She could see that his shoulder and arm were covered with bandages.

"He has lost a lot of blood," Doctor Faulkner said in a low voice, "and it is very important that he should not move about and start the wound bleeding again."

Jacoba nodded to show she understood, and the Doctor went on:

"He has had a nasty bash on the head, but fortunately they hit him not on the top but on the back."

Jacoba drew in her breath.

She knew that if the blow had been on the very

top of his head his brain could have been damaged.

"The skin was not broken," the Doctor said. "At the same time, it is a very ugly bruise which will be painful for a long time."

He replaced the sheets over the Earl's chest.

Taking Jacoba by the hand, he drew her to the window.

"You will understand," he said, "that I cannot stay here all day. I have several other patients who are very ill, and I have to attend to them."

"Yes . . . of course," Jacoba murmured.

"What I want you to do," he went on, "is to keep him quiet and make certain he does not toss and turn about, which he is very likely to want to do."

Jacoba was just going to ask how she could prevent him, when his Doctor continued:

"I have given him an herbal remedy which in my opinion is far more effective than any drug, and Cook, on my instructions, is mixing a great deal more. "If he is restless, you must make him drink it."

"I will . . . try," Jacoba promised.

"I am sure you will be very effective," the Doctor said. "You realise I have to trust you? The servants would be too afraid to gainsay him in any way."

Jacoba smiled.

"I too am frightened of him!"

"I realise that," the Doctor replied, "but you have not so much to lose as they have! You can therefore be braver and, if necessary, dictatorial!"

His eyes were twinkling, and Jacoba stifled a little laugh.

"I will do my best," she said, "but you must not expect miracles."

The Doctor put his hand on her shoulder.

"You are a good girl," he said, "and I trust you. I will be back as soon as I possibly can, but it will not be for a few hours. Ask the servants for anything you want, and I will order a footman to be always on duty outside the door."

As he spoke, he drew his watch from his pocket.

There was a look of consternation on his face.

"I must go!" he said. "And I am very thankful that I can leave you in charge."

Before Jacoba could reply, he had hurried from the room.

As he shut the door she looked across at the bed.

Incredible though it seemed, the Earl was now in her charge and she had to look after him.

She walked nearer to him and stood looking down at his white face on the pillow.

It seemed extraordinary that this man, who had shouted at her, frightened her, caused her through his anger to faint away, was now so still and silent.

Unexpectedly she found herself feeling sorry for him.

It seemed wrong that the poachers who were no more than simple thieves should have assaulted him in such a horrible fashion.

How could they have thrown him into the river?

'It was a very wicked thing to do!' Jacoba thought angrily.

She could not bear to think of such violence taking

place in the beauty of Scotland.

"You must get well," she said to the Earl, speaking without words, "and perhaps you will forget the way you have been treated and be happy again and enjoy the magnificence of your Castle."

She was not certain why this was what she wanted for him.

But she had always hated suffering and pain.

She felt it was somehow an insult to Nature, which was in itself so lovely.

"We *must* make you well!" she said to the unconscious Earl.

She knew she meant not only physically well, but also well in mind, heart, and soul.

"Then," she told herself, "he will stop hating women."

chapter six

THE Earl stirred and was vaguely aware that someone was instantly beside him.

He was being prevented from turning on his side as he wished to do.

He felt very strange and his head hurt abominably.

He wanted to ask what had happened.

Then someone gently raised his head, and a soft voice said:

"Drink this and you will feel much better. Try to drink. It will do you good."

He thought vaguely that it must be his mother who was speaking to him.

He wondered what had happened and if he had been hurt in any way.

Then darkness seemed to cover him and he slipped away into it.

* * *

"You are to go out in the fresh air," Doctor Faulkner said, "and do not come back for at least an hour-and-a-half!"

Jacoba gave a little laugh.

She was getting used to the Doctor giving her orders as if she were a raw recruit.

She knew she had to obey him.

"The Earl has been very quiet," she said, "and Angus only came to me once during the night for me to give him your herbs."

Dr. Faulkner had arranged that Angus, who was the Earl's valet, should sit up with him at night while Jacoba slept.

But she was to be with him in the daytime.

As the Doctor had a number of other very ill patients on his hands, he was unable to spend much time with the Earl.

It was now the third day that he had been unconscious.

As soon as Jacoba had gone, he and Angus redressed the Earl's wound as they did every day.

The Doctor could see it was definitely improving, and rather quicker than he had dared to hope.

"His Lordship is a strong man," he said to the valet.

He had thought, as Jacoba walked towards the door, that she looked very lovely.

The weather had grown hotter.

She was wearing a thin gown which was very simple if a little old-fashioned.

At the same time, it suited her.

Her hair with its touches of red seemed to hold the sun's rays in it.

"You are quite sure you do not need me?" she had asked before she left.

"What I am concerned with is you," he answered. "You need to be out in the fresh air and get some sunshine on your cheeks."

"I will do that," she promised.

She gave a little whistle, and the two spaniels that had been lying beside the Earl's bed jumped to their feet.

They followed her out into the corridor.

Then, as she hurried along it and down the stairs, they scampered ahead of her.

The gardens, which were very beautiful, she had already explored, as she had been able to go outside while the Doctor was dressing the Earl's wound.

Now she thought she would explore the village.

She walked up the long drive, the spaniels enjoying the walk.

They were now very friendly towards her.

She often thought when they nuzzled against her that they were apologising for having been rough when she first appeared.

The village was small and, she thought, very pretty.

It consisted of only one street in which there was a Kirk and a Post Office.

There was a Proprietor who sold groceries, and a Butcher and a Baker.

There was another shop which contained every

miscellaneous object anybody could possibly want.

At the far end of the village was a small School with a playground.

It was all very simple.

The cottages which lay directly outside the main gates of the Castle were, Jacoba was sure, occupied by the Earl's gillies as well as his Butler.

Because she had heard from the Butcher so much about his wife and family, she stopped at a gate.

It led into a pretty garden filled with flowers.

As she did so, a woman came to the door, looking at her curiously.

Jacoba smiled at her.

"I think you may be Mrs. Douglas," she said, "or perhaps she lives in one of the other cottages?"

"Ar'm Mrs. Douglas," the woman replied, "and ye'll be th' young lassie fray th' Castle."

"That is right!" Jacoba answered.

The woman came down the paved pathway and opened the gate.

"Come awa' in," she invited. "A'd like to make ye a cup o' tea."

Jacoba accepted the invitation.

She was not surprised to find that while the cottage was primitive, it was spotlessly clean.

There was a spinning-wheel at which she looked with interest.

"Ar' spin th' wool when th' sheep have been sheared," Mrs. Douglas explained, "and Ar' knit clothes for th' bairns to keep 'em warm in the winter."

"That is very clever of you," Jacoba said.

"Awl th' women mak' what they can," Mrs. Douglas said. "Money's scarce an' th' goods in th' shop are too expensive for th' lik' o' us."

Jacoba was interested.

She asked her what sort of things they made.

Mrs. Douglas ran quickly to the cottage next door.

Almost before she realised what was happening, Jacoba found herself surrounded by women.

They were all showing her what they had made and at the same time stared at her curiously.

The things they produced were certainly very cleverly done.

There were black cock's feathers fashioned into an ornament for a hat, and shells from the beach had been made into a little boat.

There were all sorts of knitted garments from slippers to bedsocks, shooting-stockings, and children's clothes.

"When th' tourists pass by, us sometimes sell things," one of the women explained, "but there's no' a lot t'see this far Norrth, except for th' Castle."

"I suppose His Lordship does not allow them inside," Jacoba said.

"Nay, nay!" they replied in shocked voices. "An' if 'e sees folk on th' drive, 'e has 'em sent awa'."

As she talked to them, Jacoba learnt how Hamish McMurdock's suggestion that they might market the lobsters and crabs had been welcomed by the local people.

"Us 'oped His Lordship would agree t' Mr. Hamish's scheme," Mrs. Douglas said.

"It would ha' put money in the fishermen's pockets, and they had a harrd time o' it last year."

"But His Lordship refused to consider it," Jacoba said as if to herself.

She was beginning to guess now why Hamish had been so angry with his uncle, why he had sent her to him as a revenge.

"Ae've hearrd," Mrs. Douglas said a little nervously, as if she were afraid she was speaking out of turn, "that ye be nurrsing His Lordship. Does he no' realise ye're doing it, and ye a lassie?"

Jacoba knew it was a question that had made them all curious.

"His Lordship is still unconscious," she said, "and I am sure when he does realise what is happening, I shall have to go away."

She rose to her feet as she spoke and added:

"That is why I want to see as much of Scotland as I can. It is so beautiful! I feel as if everything within me responds to it, and I respond to the pipes when I hear them each morning."

"How can ye say that," one woman who was more dour than the others asked. "Ye're a Sassenach, an' the Sassenachs dinna understand us."

Jacoba hesitated a moment.

Then she said quietly:

"My mother was a McKenzie. That is why I was called Jacoba."

They all stared at her.

"A McKenzie! Then ye're one o' us!"

"That is what I like to think I am," Jacoba replied.

She knew from that moment that they welcomed her amongst them.

Mrs. Douglas and two of the other women gave her presents.

Although she protested, she knew they would be hurt if she did not accept them.

"You are very kind," she said, "and I shall treasure these when I have to go back to England."

"Ye should stay here wi' us," Mrs. Douglas said. "A could teach ye t'spin, an' perhaps ye could tak' your work to Edinburgh an' earn money for it."

"That is something I would like to do," Jacoba replied.

She knew as she spoke that the little money she had would not last long.

She would have to go back to England and find a regular job.

She thanked the women for their kindness to her and walked on down the village.

When she reached the School she knew she must go back.

Doctor Faulkner had been so kind in taking her place at his patient's bedside.

She must not make him late for his next appointment.

Because she was afraid that was what she would do, she hurried down the drive, the delighted spaniels scampering along beside her.

She was breathless by the time she reached the Castle.

She ran up the stairs, pausing only to draw breath

before she opened the door into the Earl's room.

Doctor Faulkner was standing at the window, looking out to sea.

He turned as she entered.

He thought with her cheeks flushed and her hair curling over her forehead from the wind she looked like Persephone.

"I hope I have not . . . kept . . . you waiting," Jacoba said in a low voice.

"You are looking as I wanted you to look," he said. "Did you have a good time?"

"I talked to Mrs. Douglas and the other women in the cottages," Jacoba answered. "They gave me these lovely presents. I felt embarrassed at taking them, but they insisted."

"Then they have accepted you," Doctor Faulkner replied, "and they are astounded that you are here in the Castle when they have been forbidden to go near it."

Jacoba glanced towards the bed.

"How is His Lordship?"

"His arm is distinctly better," the Doctor said, "and I think he is now beginning to come back to consciousness."

"Will he be in pain?" Jacoba enquired.

"His head will still be tender and he will undoubtedly have headaches when he begins to move about. But as I have said before, he is very strong, and there will be no permanent effect from the damage."

"I am glad about that," Jacoba answered.

At the same time, she realised that if the Earl was

getting better, so the time when she could no longer stay in the Castle was approaching.

The Doctor could read what she was thinking from the expression on her face.

"I am sure His Lordship will be very grateful for what you have done for him," he said.

"I doubt it," Jacoba replied, "but, please, if you can, make him understand that . . . I cannot leave . . . unless he will . . . pay my . . . fare."

She was embarrassed at having to say it, and the colour came into her face.

Then she added:

"Of course, I could try to walk back, but I am afraid it would take a . . . very long . . . time."

The Doctor laughed.

"I expect there would be plenty of men more than willing to give you a lift!" he said. "But that is something I cannot allow."

He looked at his watch and said:

"I am late and I must be on my way. I will come back this evening, but it is not really necessary."

"Please come," Jacoba pleaded. "I am afraid, even now, that I might do something wrong."

"You are the best Nurse I have found for a long time!" the Doctor assured her.

He put his hand on her shoulder as they reached the door.

"You are to go out for at least an hour this afternoon when Angus comes on duty," he said, "and you are not to worry about His Lordship during the night. If he needs the herbs, Angus can manage."

He was gone before Jacoba could say any more.

She shut the door and went to stand beside the Earl's bed.

He was certainly looking better and was not as pale as he had been at first.

At the same time, he still looked young and exceedingly handsome.

She was suddenly aware that she did not want him to get better too quickly.

She liked nursing him, and she liked being in the Castle.

It was frightening to think she must leave it for the world outside, where nobody wanted her.

She stood looking down at the Earl for a long time.

Then, as she was about to turn away, he quite unexpectedly opened his eyes.

For a moment Jacoba could hardly believe it had happened.

Then he said in a voice that seemed to come from a long distance away:

"W-what has—happened?"

Jacoba bent a little nearer to him.

"You were hurt," she said softly, "but now you are getting well and will soon be on your feet again."

She was not certain if the Earl understood her.

After what seemed a long time, he said:

"It—it was—the—poachers."

"Yes, the poachers," Jacoba replied. "But they have gone away, and there are two men protecting the river to prevent any more coming."

She thought the earl understood.

He shut his eyes and did not speak again.

*   *   *

Jacoba went out in the afternoon just as Doctor Faulkner had told her to do, and Angus took her place in the bedroom.

She went into the garden which was just below the Castle.

A gate at the end of it led onto a stretch of level ground just above the beach.

There was a jetty jutting out into the water from which the Earl could step into a boat and row out to sea.

It was something Jacoba longed to do, especially as the sun was shining and the sea was so smooth.

She walked to the end of the jetty.

Looking down, she could see small fish swimming in the clear water, also crabs crawling in and out of the rocks which lay on the bottom.

It made her remember Hamish's idea of creating an industry and making money for the villagers.

She was well aware why the Earl would not consider such an idea.

It would mean strangers coming near him, and perhaps women.

"How can he be so foolish, when he is so young, as to cut himself off from the world?" Jacoba asked.

Yet she could guess how deeply he had been hurt by his disastrous experience at the hands of two women.

But he was wrong to hate the entire female sex.

The Doctor had told her about his unhappy marriage and about the lady who had jilted him at the last minute by running away with another man.

"It was cruel of her!" Jacoba had said.

"Yet it was better than a second unhappy marriage!" Doctor Faulkner had replied.

"I suppose that is true," Jacoba agreed.

But it was wicked to have made him look a fool, which was, of course, what any man would have felt in the same circumstances.

"I suppose the truth is," Doctor Faulkner replied, "that the Scots, despite the fact that they are strong and excellent fighters, are also very sensitive."

Jacoba did not reply.

She had not told the Doctor that her mother was a McKenzie.

In fact, she was a little surprised at herself when she admitted it to the women this morning.

It was something she had never been able to be proud of because her mother had run away with her father.

Her grandfather, whom, of course, she had never known, had been, she was told, a fanatical Jacobite.

This was the reason for her name.

He had been furious that his daughter should have married an Englishman when he hated the whole race.

He had written to his daughter, saying:

"I no longer acknowledge you as one of my family. You have disgraced our name and put a blot on our family-tree that can never be erased. I shall never mention your name again, and you are no longer fit to call yourself my daughter."

"How could he have written anything so cruel?" Jacoba asked her mother when she had shown her the letter.

"I cried for a long time after I had received it," Mrs. Ford replied, "but I knew that nothing mattered except that your father loved me and I loved him."

Her voice was very happy as she went on:

"I was so very lucky to find the only man in the world who is the other part of myself, and that is why I pray, dearest, that when you are grown-up you will do the same."

'It seems as if Mama's prayers will not be answered,' Jacoba thought despondently.

She turned from the sea and walked back towards the Castle.

When she entered the Earl's bedroom, Angus jumped up eagerly.

She knew he was bored with sitting by his unconscious master.

"Thank you very much, Angus," Jacoba said.

The spaniels went to lie beside the bed, as they always did.

Jacoba looked at the Earl to see if there was any change from when she had left.

She knew he had moved because his hand was now lying on top of the sheets.

She felt it gently to see if he was warm enough or perhaps too hot.

As she did so he opened his eyes.

"Who—are you?"

His voice made her start and she was frightened by the question.

Supposing she told him the truth and he flew into a rage? It would be very bad for him.

"I am helping Doctor Faulkner nurse you back to health," she replied finally.

The Earl was staring at her.

"Have I—seen you—before?"

Jacoba nodded.

"Yes, but do not think about it. Just try and go back to sleep."

"I am awake—have I been—asleep for—a long time?"

"This is the fourth day."

There was silence, but the Earl did not shut his eyes.

Then when she was wondering whether she should stay or go away he said:

"The poachers—hit me and something—pierced my—shoulder."

"It was a wicked thing to do!" Jacoba said. "But you are nearly well, so try and forget about it!"

There was another silence before the Earl said, and his voice sounded strange:

"I will—not have—poachers on the—river!"

"I have told you," Jacoba said patiently, "two of your men are guarding it."

The Earl gave a little sigh that was one of relief.

Then he said:

"You—have not—told me—your name."

Jacoba felt there was nothing she could do but tell him the truth.

"It is Jacoba Ford," she said quietly, "and as I am your Nurse I have to tell you not to think about anything but getting well."

"That—is what I—intend to—do," the Earl answered.

Then to her relief he shut his eyes and said no more.

* * *

When Doctor Faulkner came later in the evening, she told him what had happened.

"That confirms what I thought," he said with satisfaction, "that His Lordship has suffered no brain damage."

"I do not think he remembered that I am . . . the woman he . . . tried to . . . send away," Jacoba said.

"Well, he cannot send you away now," the Doctor said. "I shall not allow it. We still have to take care of him, and there is no one else I can put in your place."

He saw the light that came into Jacoba's eyes.

It made him aware of how afraid she was of having to leave.

As he drove away from the Castle he was wondering what he should do about her.

It was possible for him to find her some employment in the neighbourhood.

He told himself the truth was that she was too lovely.

No woman with any sense would want anything so

exquisite in her house if she had a husband or grown-up sons.

Besides that, there was not the sort of employment in this part of Scotland for somebody who was obviously a Lady.

He worried over her all the way while driving on to his next case.

He was still worrying when he came back the next morning.

As usual, he sent Jacoba away while he and Angus dressed the Earl's wound.

While they did so, the Earl had his eyes open, watching them.

When they had finished he asked briefly:

"How—soon can I—get up?"

"Perhaps in a day or so," Doctor Faulkner replied. "But even then you will not be able to leave this room. If you would like to sit up now, I will put a pillow behind you."

He and Angus lifted the Earl into a sitting position without moving his arm any more than was unavoidable.

His Lordship had already been washed and shaved.

When Jacoba came back into the room and saw him sitting up, she stared at him in surprise.

"Our patient is better!" the Doctor said.

Then before she could speak he said to the Earl:

"I cannot tell you, My Lord, how splendid Miss Ford has been in nursing you. It would have been impossible for me to manage without her, or to find anyone at a moment's notice to look after you."

The Earl did not say anything, and Jacoba held her breath.

She was so afraid he would tell her to get out of the Castle.

To her surprise he said:

"Of course I am grateful, but now I would like something substantial to eat. I am also very thirsty."

"That is the best news I have heard for days," Doctor Faulkner said, "and I know Miss Ford would like to carry the good news to Cook."

Jacoba knew he was giving her the chance to leave the room.

She went down to the kitchens.

She had already made friends with Cook, who had been at the Castle for years.

He had originally been employed as a young man to help the old Cook.

Mrs. Sutherland had been an important part of the household.

She had looked after the Earl's father for over thirty years.

She had been on the point of retiring when the Earl had given orders that there were to be no women in the Castle.

No woman should ever enter it again.

Mrs. Sutherland had asked to see the Earl, but he had refused.

"A'd like to give Master Tarbot a piece of my mind!" she had said. "But there, that's what ye get for a' the years A've slaved awa' making his favourite dishes since he was in the pram!"

Being banned from the Castle, she was very resentful at not being able to pop into the kitchens.

She wanted to talk to the man who had taken her place, and help mix the Christmas pudding.

It had always been a tradition that everybody in the Castle should have a stir of it for good luck.

Euan, the man who had taken her place, welcomed Jacoba with a slight smile.

He was a kindly man and a very good Cook, and was always conscientious about his work.

She told him what the Earl wanted.

He started immediately to cook one of his favourite dishes that would not take too long.

Jacoba thanked him and went off to the Pantry to find Douglas.

He was polishing some of the fine silver which he put on the table for her to admire.

"His Lordship is thirsty and has asked for a drink!" she told him.

"Then 'e be on th' men'," Douglas remarked.

"That is true," Jacoba replied. "What are you going to give him?"

"A' thinks this calls for a glass o' champagne!" Douglas answered. "Us 'as a few bottles left over from last Christmas, an' A'm sure th' Doctor 'll fancy a wee drop, an' so 'll ye, Miss Jacoba."

"I would not refuse!" Jacoba laughed. "But I suspect His Lordship would be horrified at my drinking it, so please keep it for me until dinner."

As she spoke she wondered how long it would be before she would sit for the last time at the magnificent table or eat such delicious food served by Douglas and one of the footmen.

As if he knew what she was thinking, Douglas asked:

"His Lordship hasna sent ye awa'?"

"The Doctor made it clear it was important I should stay."

Douglas smiled.

"That be guid news, verry guid news, Miss Jacoba!"

Almost reluctantly Jacoba went upstairs again.

She had no idea that as soon as she had left the room, Doctor Faulkner had said to the Earl:

"Now, whatever you may be feeling about Jacoba, I will not have you upsetting yourself over her!"

He had wondered as he spoke if the Earl realised who Jacoba was.

He was almost certain he did, and when the Earl spoke again he knew he was right.

"She was unable to go before I was assaulted by those poachers," the Earl said as if he were reasoning it out for himself, "so I suppose you told her to stay."

"I begged her to do so," Doctor Faulkner answered. "When you were brought back to the Castle badly injured and half-drowned, I could not have managed without her."

"Half-drowned?" the Earl enquired.

"The poachers made sure you could not give evidence against them," the Doctor answered, "by throwing you in the river in the hope you would drown!"

There was a pause before the Earl said:

"I find it hard to believe that that sort of thing can happen on the Tavor!"

"Well, it did," the Doctor replied, "but it is something which should not happen again."

"I will make sure of that as soon as I am up and about," the Earl said.

"I hope you will, but you have to get well slowly, and you still require careful nursing, do not forget that!"

The Earl did not reply.

But there was a twist to his lips which told the Doctor, who was very perceptive, that he was well aware why he was speaking so positively.

When Jacoba came back into the room, he made no comment.

He merely listened when she told the Doctor that Euan was cooking something quickly for the Earl.

She also told him that Douglas was bringing up something to quench his thirst.

As she finished speaking, Douglas appeared with the champagne.

Although she thought the Earl raised his eye-brows at the sight of it, he did not say anything.

"Champagne!" the Doctor remarked as Douglas offered him a glass. "This certainly calls for a celebration! Your Lordship is better, your shoulder is nearly healed, and you can thank God that your brain was undamaged."

The Earl looked at him questioningly.

"Was that a possibility?"

"Definitely so!" the Doctor said. "They hit you

with something hard and heavy, probably an oar."

"Then, of course, I can say only that I am very thankful, both to Fate and to you, certainly, Doctor!"

He paused, and then as if it were with an effort, he added:

"—and to Miss Ford!"

Jacoba felt shy.

Then the Earl said sharply to Douglas:

"A glass of champagne for Miss Ford!"

Douglas went outside the door and came back with a glass in his hand.

Jacoba knew he had brought it upstairs.

She took the glass of champagne in her hand, and the Doctor said:

"I think, Jacoba, you and I should drink to His Lordship. Shall I give the toast?"

"Y-yes . . . of course," Jacoba replied.

The Doctor raised his glass.

"To the Chieftain! That he will soon be well, and may he find happiness in the future and prosperity for the Clan!"

Jacoba thought it was a daring toast.

Then to her astonishment the Earl did not scowl or express any disapproval.

Instead, he said:

"Thank you, Faulkner."

But he was looking at Jacoba.

As she raised her glass his eyes met hers and she could not look away.

She felt a strange sensation in her breast which she had never felt before.

She did not understand it, but she was suddenly breathless, as if she had been running.

And at the same time, the room seemed filled with sunshine.

chapter seven

ALL through the next two days Jacoba was aware that the Earl was watching her.

He did not say anything.

He accepted that she looked after him and did everything the Doctor had ordered her to do.

At the same time, she had the uneasy feeling that he was like a tiger waiting to spring.

'I shall have to leave,' she thought despairingly at night when she was in her own room.

Then she knew that every day she was in Scotland she loved it more.

The beauty of it seemed to seep into her, and she felt it would be an intolerable wrench when she finally had to say goodbye.

The Doctor had ordered that she should massage very gently the Earl's forehead.

It was to move the blood which he was afraid might

have clotted where the deep bruise had been.

At first Jacoba was shy of touching him while he was awake.

Then she told herself that as a Nurse she must be impersonal.

It would be foolish to have any particular feelings about what she had to do.

The Earl submitted to her massage by closing his eyes and lying very still.

She was very gentle, her fingers moving softly and rhythmically over his forehead, and the first time she did it he fell asleep.

In the evening, as she had to do it twice a day, he remained awake.

When she had finished he just said:

"Thank you."

She knew that not only every day, but every hour he seemed to be getting better and stronger.

He was allowed to sit in a warm robe at the open window.

There he would either look out at the exquisite view over the sea, or else he would read the newspapers.

Even when he was reading, Jacoba was conscious, although she thought she must be wrong, that he was watching her as she moved about his room.

She had the terrifying feeling that he was sorting out in his mind exactly what he would say when he told her to go.

She wanted to discuss what she should do with Doctor Faulkner.

But he had, as he had said, two or three desperate cases on his hands.

He came into the Castle in a hurry, saw the Earl, then left again.

'I must talk to him,' she thought.

Then she knew she had in fact nothing to say.

She lay awake at night, wondering whom she should approach in the village at home when she returned.

She remembered that the Viscount had told her to get in touch with him.

However, she thought that would be a mistake.

The one thing she did not want was to have to tell him and Hamish McMurdock the way his uncle had behaved when she first arrived at the Castle.

It was embarrassing to think of it even to herself.

She knew she could not bear to speak of it either to Hamish or to the Viscount.

This morning when she awoke she was told that he was getting up.

He did not require her services.

She had expected to have a message something like that.

Yet when Douglas gave it to her she felt as if she had received a blow on the head.

"M' wife was hopin', Miss," Douglas said, "that ye'd drop by an' see her. She's somethin' tae show ye which she thinks might be o' interest."

"Is it something she has made?" Jacoba asked with an effort.

"That it is, Miss," Douglas affirmed.

Jacoba thought sadly that when she was gone there would be nobody to be interested in what the women made, or to think of ways to sell their wares.

'There is so much I could do here,' she murmured.

Then she was aware that she was tempting herself to find an excuse to stay.

She knew that she could not offend the Earl by remaining in the neighbourhood.

To her surprise, the Earl did not send for her before luncheon.

She would have gone out into the garden had there not been a heavy sea mist.

It was not raining, but she was sure the skies were dark and the mist became thicker as the day wore on.

She had luncheon alone in the Dining-Room.

Only when she had finished it did Douglas say:

"His Lorrdship'd like a worrd wi' ye, Miss, in the Study."

She had a feeling this was ominous, but she could not say anything to Douglas.

She got up from the table and walked slowly across the landing before she opened the door of the Study.

She knew her hand was trembling.

She told herself she must be more sensible.

The Earl was standing in front of the fireplace.

He was wearing the kilt and looked as imposing, she thought, as the portrait of his father above the mantelpiece.

Slowly she closed the door behind her and walked towards him.

When he did not speak she said:

"I am . . . so glad you are . . . better but you must not . . . do too much."

"I am perfectly well," the Earl replied in a hard voice.

He did not ask Jacoba to sit down.

She waited, feeling as if she were standing in the dock.

She was about to receive punishment for some crime she had committed.

"I am, of course, exceedingly grateful to you, Miss Ford," the Earl said slowly, "for the way you have looked after me while I have been ill. But I know you will understand that there is now no necessity for me to have a Nurse, and, of course, you will wish to leave."

Jacoba made a little murmur, but she did not speak, and after a minute he continued:

"I have arranged to reimburse you for your services. I think you will find I have acted generously in the matter, and I have also included your fare back to London."

His voice was hard.

As he finished speaking he turned round to look at the fireplace as if he could not bear the sight of her.

Suddenly something seemed to snap in Jacoba.

She made a sound like an animal caught in a trap.

Without thinking, as if driven by some force within her, she ran from the room, down the stairs, and out through the front-door.

She ran up the drive, and crossing the road she

took a twisting footpath which she had seen before and which led up to the moors.

She did not stop to think where she was going or what she was doing.

She knew only that the Earl was sending her away from everything that mattered to her, everything that was now a part of her life, and she could not bear it.

On and on she went.

She saw only the twisting path at her feet because the sea mist obscured the moors and the valley that led down to the sea.

She climbed and climbed until she was too exhausted to go any farther.

It was then she stumbled over a rock and fell headlong into the heather.

She did not get up but merely started to cry despairingly and hopelessly.

There was nothing left but a world in which she had no place.

It was a world she could not see, a world that enveloped her obscurely, and she wanted only to die.

Even as she cried she knew she was crying not only for herself, or for the hopeless position she was in, but because she loved the Earl.

* * *

When Jacoba had gone, the Earl stood looking into the fire without turning.

The door was half ajar, and he did not move even

when he heard somebody come into the room.

There was a pause before Doctor Faulkner exclaimed:

"You are up, My Lord! That is good news! How are you feeling?"

"I am all right," the Earl said curtly, as if he disliked answering questions.

Doctor Faulkner walked towards the fireplace.

"I am damp and cold," he said. "If there is one thing I dislike, it is a sea mist."

The Earl did not answer, and the Doctor continued:

"I hope Miss Ford has not gone out in this weather. If it catches her throat, I shall have another invalid on my hands!"

Still the Earl did not say anything, and after a moment the Doctor enquired:

"Where is Miss Ford, by the way?"

"She ran out of the room and I heard her going down the stairs, I presume to go into the garden."

Doctor Faulkner stared at the Earl.

"Why did she run out of the room? Have you upset her?"

"I told her she had to leave," the Earl explained. "I have written out an extremely large cheque to pay for her services, and included the price of her ticket to London."

The Doctor was silent. Then he said:

"Then it *was* Jacoba I saw running across the road and up the path to the moor. I thought I must be mistaken.

"What are you talking about?" the Earl asked.

"She should not be going up on the moor in this mist," the Doctor said, "but I suppose, as you have sent her away, she has gone somewhere to cry unobserved."

"To cry?" the Earl asked. "Why should she want to do that?"

"Oh, for God's sake, man!" the Doctor said impatiently. "The girl has been with you ever since you became conscious. You cannot be so stupid as not to realise that she is in love with you!"

The Earl stared at him.

"In love with—me? Why should you think that?"

"I have eyes in my head," the Doctor said, "and I had hoped, although, of course, it was extremely foolish of me, that perhaps, as she is such an exceptional person and so beautiful, she might turn you into a human being!"

There was a defeated note in his voice as he added:

"But I was mistaken, and God knows what will happen to her now if she gets lost on the moor!"

As he was speaking he was aware that the Earl was staring at him in a strange manner.

Without saying a word he went from the room.

The Doctor heard his footsteps running down the stairs.

*　　*　　*

Jacoba was aware that the mist which covered her was damp and cold, but somehow it did not seem to matter.

148

Her hands were still covering her face as she cried, but no longer as convulsively as she had before.

Now she cried tears of despair, the tears of someone who has lost all hope.

The world was lost and she was abandoned in a "No-man's-land."

She thought if she died here, no one would find her.

The Earl would merely be glad that she had gone and he need no longer be troubled by her.

It was then she became aware of something nuzzling against her.

As she started, suddenly frightened, she realised it was one of the Earl's spaniels.

The dog began to bark, and the other spaniel, who must have been just behind him, came running up, also barking.

Jacoba put out a shaking hand towards them.

As she did so, she became aware that somebody large and dark was looming up through the mist.

Even as she looked up, the Earl knelt down beside her and put his arms around her.

Jacoba gave a little gasp as he pulled her against him, saying:

"How could you run away like that? How could you do anything so foolish as to climb the moors alone in the mist?"

She thought he was angry.

At the same time, she felt her heart turn a somersault because he was there and his arms were around her.

She hid her face against his shoulder.

"How could you leave me?" he asked. "Supposing I had not been able to find you?"

Jacoba thought she must be dreaming.

Yet there was a note in his voice she had never heard before.

"Y-you . . . told me to . . . go away," she said in a voice that was little above a whisper.

"That was because I thought after the way I treated you when you first arrived that you must hate me!"

He put his hand under her chin to turn her face up to his.

They could only just see each other through the mist, and yet she was vividly aware of him and how close he was.

"What do you feel about me?" he asked. "Tell me, tell me the truth, for I could not bear anything else."

Because it did not seem real, Jacoba could only answer:

"I . . . I love you . . . I love you . . . I cannot help it . . . and . . . if I have to . . . go away . . . I would . . . r-rather . . . die!"

The Earl's arms tightened until it was difficult for her to breathe.

Then he was kissing her, kissing her not gently but fiercely, demandingly, as if he were afraid of losing her and was fighting the world to keep her with him.

She could not believe it was happening.

Yet as his lips took possession of hers she felt as if a shaft of lightning flashed through her.

It was a rapture, and half a pain.

It was so intense, so different from anything she

had ever known before, she could hardly believe it was real and not part of a dream.

The Earl was kissing her, but now he was more gentle, yet still demanding and possessive, and she loved him with her whole being.

It was true that if she could not stay with him, she would rather die.

Only when a long time later he raised his head did she say incoherently:

"Please let me . . . stay . . . please let me be . . . near you!"

"You will stay with me for ever!" the Earl said.

"Are . . . are you . . . sure?"

"I love you! I love you as I have never loved anyone before! But I was so desperately afraid that you must hate me that I had to send you away."

He did not wait for her to answer, but kissed her again.

He kissed her until she thought she must have died and had somehow reached Heaven.

A long time later the Earl said:

"Come, I must take you back, my darling. It is dangerous to be out in this mist."

Jacoba looked up at him and gave a little laugh.

"The mist has . . . lifted!"

The Earl raised his head and saw that she was right.

While he had been kissing her, crouched in the heather with the two dogs lying beside them, the mist had lifted.

The sky had lightened.

There was just a glimmer of sunlight.

151

Looking back, they could see the towers of the Castle, but there was still some mist hovering over the woods and the garden, but that too was dispersing.

The Earl rose to his feet and pulled Jacoba to hers.

With his arms round her he said:

"How can you be so beautiful! Do you really love me?"

"I . . . love you . . . and I am . . . so happy that I am . . . sure I am . . . dreaming!" Jacoba replied.

The Earl kissed her eyes as if he would kiss away the tears that had made her lashes wet.

Then he said:

"I am taking you home, and you must have a hot bath immediately in case you catch a chill."

Jacoba gave a little cry.

"That is something you too must avoid when you have been so ill!"

She put out her hands to touch him.

"How could . . . you have come . . . out into . . . the mist to . . . find me?"

"Because otherwise I might have lost you," the Earl said. "Now, come along, darling, let us talk about it when we get home."

He took her by the hand, and they walked down the twisting path.

It was so steep that Jacoba wondered how she had managed to climb so high when she could see nothing beyond where she put her feet.

The spaniels raced ahead of them.

They were wagging their tails as if they knew that everything was all right.

As the Castle came into view Jacoba said:

"I am soaking wet and I am . . . sure I look . . . awful! I do not want anyone to see . . . me like . . . this."

The Earl smiled.

"You look lovely to me, but I know what you mean. We will go in by a side-door."

They went in through one which opened onto the garden and up a different staircase from the main one at the front of the Castle.

The Earl took her to her room and as he opened the door he said:

"Hurry, because I want to talk to you. I will be in my Study."

He would have gone away, but Jacoba said:

"You must get out of those clothes. You too are wet!"

"Are you still looking after me?" the Earl asked.

"I am still . . . your Nurse . . . and therefore . . . you must . . . obey me!"

He laughed before he said:

"I will obey you and you will obey me. I will tell the servants to bring you up a bath of hot water."

"You are to have one too!" Jacoba answered. "I would not want you to be ill again."

There was so much love in her voice that the Earl took a step towards her.

Then, as if he knew she was right in thinking they

153

must both take off their wet clothes, he went to his own room.

Jacoba took off all her clothes which were very wet.

She got into bed aware she was shivering.

At the same time, her heart was surging with happiness.

The bath was brought into her bedroom and the hot water arrived surprisingly quickly.

She bathed, dressed, and was in such a hurry to get back to the Earl that she hardly looked in the mirror.

She ran along the passage and found, as he had said, that he was in his Study.

She opened the door, and for a moment they just looked at each other.

Then the Earl held out his arms and she ran towards him.

He held her close and as she looked up at him he said:

"I love you, my darling! We are going to be married to-morrow, or at the very latest, the day after."

"M-married?" Jacoba stammered.

"I intend to tie you to me by every vow and law that exists," the Earl said.

Jacoba gave what was almost a little sob and hid her face against him.

"I . . . I am not . . . grand enough to be your . . . wife," she whispered. "And suppose . . . after we are married you are . . . disappointed?"

The Earl laughed, and it was a very tender sound.

"You are everything I have ever wanted," he said, "and nobody will stop me from having you with me every day, every hour, and every second for the rest of our lives!"

Then he was kissing her again, kissing her demandingly, so that she knew he intended, whatever the difficulties, to have his own way.

Her eyes were shining and he only released her to say:

"I am being selfish! I should have given you something to drink as soon as we got back to the Castle. To make quite sure, my lovely one, that you do not catch cold, I want you to drink a little brandy."

He walked to the table in the corner as he spoke.

He brought back a glass he had already prepared for her.

She wrinkled her nose.

"I know it is . . . very strong . . . and I do not . . . like it."

"But you will drink it, to please me," the Earl said.

She looked up at him.

"You know I want to . . . please you, and I will do . . . anything you say."

She drank a little of the brandy as she spoke and looked at him questioningly.

"A little more!" he insisted.

She could feel it seeping through her.

It swept away the last vestiges of the wet and chilling mist.

He took the glass from her and put it down on a table.

When he came back she was holding out her hands to the fire.

The flames were leaping up the big chimney.

"There is so much I want to say to you," he said, "but when I look at you all I want to do is to kiss you and ask you again and again if you love me."

"If I tell you . . . how much perhaps . . . you will grow . . . tired of hearing it."

He pulled her against him, but as his lips sought hers the door opened.

Douglas seemed to burst into the room.

The Earl and Jacoba both looked round.

"M'Lord! M'Lord!" Douglas exclaimed. "There's trouble, I'm afraid."

"Trouble?" the Earl enquired.

"It's the women, M'Lord. They're at the front-door demandin' tae see ye. Ma ain wife's among them, an' I'm not able to stop her."

"I cannot imagine what this is all about," the Earl exclaimed.

"A' think ye should come at once, M'Lord," Douglas said.

The Earl walked from the Study.

Because she was curious and also a little apprehensive, Jacoba followed him.

He went down the stairs and she could see in the hall there were two footmen barring the way to the women outside.

It was growing late.

Dusk had come and there was still a mist over the garden and the lower part of the Castle.

Keeping in the background as the Earl walked towards the door, Jacoba could see through the window that there was a large crowd of women outside.

Behind them there were a number of men looking, she thought, a little shamefaced and upset by what was occurring.

The two footmen moved to one side.

The Earl walked outside to stand at the top of the steps looking down at the women.

"You wanted to see me?" he asked in a clear voice.

A woman moved forward.

Jacoba recognised her as the one who had questioned as to why a Sassenach should be interested in Scotland.

She stood facing the Earl and said:

"Aye, we've come t'tell ye we've had enough o' your curses. Mrs. McAllister's lost her wee son this mornin', an' Ferguson's found his best ewe dead in t'road."

She drew in her breath. There was a little murmur of agreement among the other women before their spokeswoman went on:

" 'Tis ye, M'Lord, who's brought this trouble upon us, an' noo we hear ye've sent awa' yon lassie who nursed ye back t'health. She's one o' us, an' 'tis ye who should be leavin'—not her!

"We've come t'tell ye noo that we'll choose another Chieftain, an' either ye go, or we'll burrn doon the Castle, an' wi' it your curses!"

She seemed almost to spit the words at the Earl.

Now the other women lifted up their arms and shouted:

"Get oot! Go! Awa' an' leave us in peace!"

They sounded so truculent and savage that for one frightening moment Jacoba thought they might rush at the Earl and injure him.

Instinctively she moved forward to stand at his side.

As she appeared there was a gasp.

She knew that the women believed she had gone, or perhaps the rumour had spread that she was lost on the moors.

She slipped her hand into the Earl's.

She knew he was feeling for words and trying to think of how he could answer the angry women who faced him.

Before he could say anything Jacoba said:

"You have got it wrong. Everything has changed . . . and if there have been curses put on you they have now been . . . swept away by something much stronger than evil, and that is . . . Love!"

She blushed a little as she spoke and looked at the Earl.

His fingers tightened on hers as he said, and his voice seemed to ring out:

"That is true, and I know you will congratulate me when you hear that I have asked Jacoba Ford to be my wife. I now invite you all to our wedding, which will take place the day after to-morrow!"

For a moment the women were silent from sheer astonishment.

Then they started to cheer.

Their voices rang out and seemed to echo, then re-echo round the Castle.

The men began to cheer too and the Earl held out his hand so that those nearest to him could shake it.

As they did so, the Earl's Piper, as if inspired by what he had heard, started up his pipes.

It was the song of the Clan.

As they all began to sing it, Jacoba found the tears were running down her face.

But now they were tears of happiness and she knew that everything she wanted for the Clan would come true.

She and the Earl would lead them to a prosperity that they had never known before.

* * *

It was a long time later before Jacoba and the Earl could go back into the Castle, but not before they had shaken hands with everybody.

When she could speak Jacoba said:

"I still cannot . . . believe that the women would . . . really have sent . . . you away."

"Curses are very powerful in Scotland," the Earl replied, "but so are blessings, and that is what you have brought me, my precious, a blessing I will never lose."

"I . . . I hope that . . . is true," Jacoba said, "but—"

Before she could go on the Earl interrupted:

"Because I can read your thoughts, I know you are thinking of all the things I should have done for the Clan, which with your help I shall do now."

"Do . . . you mean . . . that?" Jacoba asked excitedly.

"I think, as Hamish sent you to me, we should thank him," the Earl said simply, "and he can organise the sale of the lobsters and crabs in London as he planned, but I intend to take particular interest in how it works from this end."

Jacoba gave a cry of delight.

"That will help bring . . . prosperity to your people."

The Earl's eyes twinkled.

"I know without your telling me that you have dozens of other ideas in mind, and of course I must see you are kept busy in case you become bored with me."

"I shall . . . never do . . . that," Jacoba said. "How could anyone be as wonderful as you, and make me . . . feel as I . . . do now!"

"What do you feel?" the Earl asked.

"So much . . . in love that it is . . . impossible to . . . put it into . . . words what I feel when . . . you kiss . . . me—"

"You have never been kissed before?"

"Of course not!"

The Earl laughed.

"Because you are so lovely I have tortured myself with the thought of the men who kiss you when you are in London."

"I have been in London only once . . . and that

was the night . . . before I . . . came to . . . Scotland," Jacoba said.

There was a shy expression in her eyes as she went on:

"I . . . I do not think . . . you realise how . . . ignorant I am of . . . anything other than . . . the English countryside. I have . . . met very few men and certainly . . . never one . . . like you!"

"That is exactly how it should be!" the Earl declared. "Exactly what I want in my wife, and what the McMurdocks want in their Chieftain's wife."

Then as he swept her into his arms he said:

"I love you, my darling! I vow I will make you happy and nothing else shall ever hurt us again."

She knew as his lips found hers that he was thinking of how hurt he had been in the past.

She vowed that she would never disappoint him or do anything to make him unhappy.

She knew too that it was her prayers which had brought her safely to Scotland.

It was her prayers that had prevented the Earl from sending her back South.

He carried her once again up to a special Heaven of their own.

As he did so, she was thanking God for giving her the only thing in life that really mattered.

That was Love.

Barbara Cartland, the world's most famous romantic novelist, who is also an historian, playwright, lecturer, political speaker and television personality, has now written over 520 books and sold over 500 million copies all over the world.

She has also had many historical works published and has written four autobiographies as well as the biographies of her mother and that of her brother, Ronald Cartland, who was the first Member of Parliment to be killed in the last war. This book has a preface by Sir Winston Churchill and has just been republished with an introduction by Sir Arthur Bryant.

Love at the Helm, a novel written with the help and inspiration of the late Earl Mountbatten of Burma, Great Uncle of His Royal Highness The Prince of Wales, is being sold for the Mountbatten Memorial Trust.

She has broken the world record for the last fourteen years by writing an average of twenty-three books a year. In the *Guinness Book of Records* she is listed as the world's top-selling author.

Miss Cartland in 1978 sang an Album of Love Songs with the Royal Philharmonic Orchestra.

In private life Barbara Cartland, who is a Dame of

the Order of St. John of Jerusalem, Chairman of the St. John Council in Hertfordshire and Deputy President of the St. John Ambulance Brigade, has fought for better conditions and salaries for Midwives and Nurses.

She championed the cause for the Elderly in 1956 invoking a Government Enquiry into the "Housing Conditions of Old People."

In 1962 she had the Law of England changed so that Local Authorities had to provide camps for their own Gypsies. This has meant that since then thousands and thousands of Gypsy children have been able to go to School, which they had never been able to do in the past, as their caravans were moved every twenty-four hours by the Police.

There are now fourteen camps in Hertfordshire and Barbara Cartland has her own Romany Gypsy Camp called Barbaraville by the Gypsies.

Her designs "Decorating with Love" are being sold all over the U.S.A. and the National Home Fashions League made her, in 1981, "Woman of Achievement."

She is unique in that she was one and two in the Dalton list of Best Sellers, and one week had four books in the top twenty.

Barbara Cartland's book *Getting Older, Growing Younger* has been published in Great Britain and the U.S.A. and her fifth cookery book, *The Romance of Food*, is now being used by the House of Commons.

In 1984 she received at Kennedy Airport America's Bishop Wright Air Industry Award for her contribution to the development of aviation. In 1931 she and two R.A.F. Officers thought of, and carried, the first aeroplane-towed glider airmail.

During the War she was Chief Lady Welfare Officer in Bedfordshire looking after 20,000 Service men and women. She thought of having a pool of Wedding Dresses at the War Office so a Service Bride could hire a gown for the day.

She bought 1,000 gowns without coupons for the A.T.S., the W.A.A.F.'s and the W.R.E.N.S. In 1945 Barbara Cartland received the Certificate of Merit from Eastern Command.

In 1964 Barbara Cartland founded the National Association for Health of which she is the President, as a front for all the Health Stores and for any product made as alternative medicine.

This is now a £65 million turnover a year, with one third going in export.

In January 1988 she received *La Médaille de Vermeil de la Ville de Paris*. This is the highest award to be given in France by the City of Paris. She has sold 25 million books in France.

In March 1988 Barbara Cartland was asked by the Indian Government to open their Health Resort outside Delhi. This is almost the largest Health Resort in the world.

Barbara Cartland was received with great enthusiasm by her fans, who fêted her at a reception in the City, and she received the gift of an embossed plate from the Government.